WHO WILL SURVIVE?

IT'S GOING TO BE A KILLER YEAR!

Is the senior class at Shadyside High doomed? That's the prediction Trisha Conrad makes at her summer party—and it looks as if she may be right. Spend a year with the FEAR STREET seniors, as each month in this new 12-book series brings horror after horror. Will anyone reach graduation day alive?

Only R.L. Stine knows…

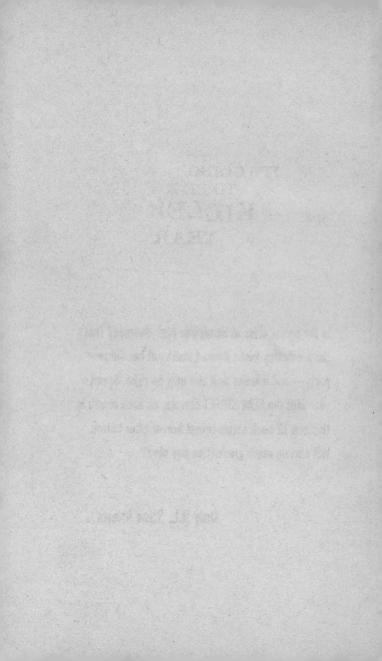

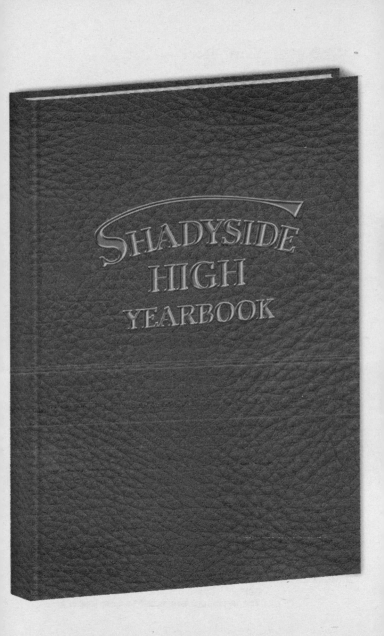

SHADYSIDE HIGH YEARBOOK

Mira Block

LIKES:
Going to clubs, guys in bands, sexy clothes

REMEMBERS:
The cemetery, senior camp-out, hanging out with Clarissa

HATES:
Waifs, talking on the phone, psychics

QUOTE:
"Don't hate me 'cause I'm beautiful."

Greta Bradley

LIKES:
Cheerleading, looking cool, all my cool friends

REMEMBERS:
The first time Ty asked me out, shopping at Chanel with Jade

HATES:
Ceramics, cheap shoes, New Year's

QUOTE:
"That boy is mine."

Trisha Conrad

LIKES:
Shopping in the mall my dad owns, giving fabulous parties, Gary Fresno

REMEMBERS:
The murder game, the senior table at Pete's Pizza

HATES:
Rich girl jokes, bad karma, overalls

QUOTE:
"What you don't know will hurt you."

Danielle Cortez

LIKES:
My cute outfits, cheering for the Tigers, dancing

REMEMBERS:
Trisha's party, finally making varsity cheerleader

HATES:
The first day of school, being cold, overalls

QUOTE:
"Push 'em down, push 'em down, push 'em waaaay down! Go Tigers!"

Clark Dickson

LIKES:
Debra Lake, poetry, painting

REMEMBERS:
Trisha's party, the first time I saw Debra

HATES:
Nicknames, dentists, garlic pizza, tans

QUOTE:
"Fangs for the memories."

Jennifer Fear

LIKES:
Basketball, antique jewelry, cool music

REMEMBERS:
The doom spell, senior cut day, hanging with Trisha and Josie

HATES:
The way people are afraid of the Fears, pierced eyebrows

QUOTE:
"There's nothing to fear but fear itself."

Jade Feldman

LIKES:
Cheerleading, expensive clothes, working out

REMEMBERS:
Ice skates and gab fests with Deena

HATES:
Cheerleading tryouts, losers, SAT prep courses

QUOTE:
"You get what you pay for."

Gary Fresno

LIKES:
Hanging out by the bleachers, art class, gym

REMEMBERS:
Cruisin' down Division Street with the guys, that special night with that special person (you know who you are...)

HATES:
My beat-up Civic, working after school everyday, cops

QUOTE:
"Don't judge a book by its cover."

Kenny Klein

LIKES:
Jade Feldman, chemistry, Latin, baseball

REMEMBERS:
The first time I beat Marla Newman in a debate, Junior Prom with Jade

HATES:
Nine-year-olds who like to torture camp counselors, cafeteria food

QUOTE:
"Look before you leap."

Debra Lake

LIKES:
Sensitive ~~guys~~, Clark's poetry

REMEMBERS:
Basketball games, when Clark painted my portrait

HATES:
Possessive boyfriends and jealous girlfriends

QUOTE:
"I would do anything for you, but I won't do that."

REST IN PEACE

Stacy Malcolm

LIKES:
Sports, funky hats, shopping

REMEMBERS:
Running laps with Mary, stuffing our faces at Pete's, Mr. Morley and Rob

HATES:
Psycho killers, stealing boyfriends

QUOTE:
"College, here I come!"

Josh Maxwell

LIKES:
Debra Lake, Debra Lake, Debra Lake

REMEMBERS:
Hanging out at the old mill, senior camp-out, Coach's pep talks

HATES:
Funeral homes, driving my parents' car, tomato juice

QUOTE:
"Sometimes you don't realize the truth until it bites you right on the neck."

Josie Maxwell

LIKES:
Black clothes, black nail polish, black lipstick, photography

REMEMBERS:
Trisha's first senior party, the memorial wall

HATES:
Algebra, evil spirits (including Marla Newman), being compared to my stepbrother Josh

QUOTE:
"The past isn't always the past—sometimes it's the future."

Mickey Myers

LIKES:
Jammin' with the band, partying, hot girls

REMEMBERS:
Swimming in Fear Lake, the storm, my first gig at the Underground

HATES:
Dweebs, studying, girls who diet, station wagons

QUOTE:
"Shadyside High rules!"

Marla Newman

LIKES:
Writing, cool clothes, being a redhead

REMEMBERS:
Yearbook deadlines, competing with Kenny Klein, when Josie put a spell on me (ha ha)

HATES:
Girls who wear all black, guys with long hair, the dark arts

QUOTE:
"The power is divided when the circle is not round."

Mary O'Connor

LIKES:
Running, ripped jeans, hair spray

REMEMBERS:
Not being invited to Trisha's party, rat poison

HATES:
Social studies, rich girls, cliques

QUOTE:
"Just say no."

Dana Palmer

LIKES:
Boys, boys, boys, cheerleading, short skirts

REMEMBERS:
Senior camp-out with Mickey, Homecoming, the back seat

HATES:
Private cheerleading performances, fire batons, sharing clothes

QUOTE:
"The bad twin always wins!"

Deirdre Palmer

LIKES:
My friends, sharing things, guys, our movies

REMEMBERS:
The cabin in the Fear Street woods, sleepovers at Jen's

HATES:
Being a "good girl," sweat socks

QUOTE:
"What you see isn't always what you get."

Will Reynolds

LIKES:
The Turner family, playing guitar, clubbing

REMEMBERS:
The first time Clarissa saw me without my dreads, our booth at Pete's

HATES:
Lite FM, the clinic, lilacs

QUOTE:
"I get knocked down, but I get up again…"

Ty Sullivan

LIKES:
Cheerleaders with tosses, fears, swains, brains, football

REMEMBERS:
The back yard with you know who, Klein's lucky shot

HATES:
Painting faces, the bus bay

QUOTE:
"The more the merrier."

Justin Thompson

LIKES:
Computers, Nintendo, Marilyn Manson, Beastie Boys, Barry White

REMEMBERS:
Don't want to remember anything about Bradyside

HATES:
Having my head stuck in the toilet, being chased by Ty and Gary

QUOTE:
"You're my everything."

Clarissa Turner

LIKES:
Art, music, talking on the phone

REMEMBERS:
Shopping with Debra, my first day back to school, eating pizza with Will

HATES:
Mira Block

QUOTE:
"Real friendship never dies."

Matty Winger

LIKES:
Computers, video games, Star Trek

REMEMBERS:
The murder game—good one Trisha

HATES:
People who can't take a joke, finding Clark's cape with Josh

QUOTE:
"Don't worry, be happy."

Phoebe Yamura

LIKES:
Cheerleading, gymnastics, big crowds

REMEMBERS:
That awesome game against Waynesbridge, senior trip, tailgate parties

HATES:
When people don't give it their all, liars, vans

QUOTE:
"Today is the first day of the rest of our lives."

Wicked

R.L. Stine
Seniors
a FEAR STREET series

episode ten Wicked

A Parachute Press Book

A GOLD KEY PAPERBACK
Golden Books Publishing Company, Inc.
New York

Check out the new FEAR STREET® Website
http://www.fearstreet.com

A Gold Key Paperback Original

Golden Books Publishing Company, Inc.
888 Seventh Avenue
New York, NY 10106

ISBN: 0-307-24714-7

First Gold Key paperback printing April 1999

10 9 8 7 6 5 4 3 2 1

Photographer: Jimmy Levin

Printed in the U.S.A.

Wicked

Melanie Anderson leaned toward the mirror, brushing out her long, straight black hair. She tilted her head to one side, watching the hair shimmer into place.

My best feature, she thought.

Everyone says my hair could sell shampoo on TV commercials. It's because I take care of it. I don't use those harsh shampoos. I don't—

She stopped with a sharp gasp—and stared at the mirror, at the face that appeared behind her.

"You're here?" Melanie cried, spinning around.

No. No one standing behind her.

But the face—?

Her heart racing, Melanie turned back to the

1

mirror. And saw *two* other faces smiling out at her.

Two faces she recognized. Two faces she dreaded.

Not with her in her room. They grinned out at her, only in the mirror.

"What are you doing here? What do you *want*?" Melanie cried, unable to hide her terror.

She *knew* what they wanted.

"No!" Melanie screamed angrily. "Leave me alone! Leave me alone!" She smashed her fist against the glass.

But the grins on the two girls' faces didn't fade.

"Get out of my room!" Melanie shrieked. "Get out of my mirror!"

The faces stared out at her, as real, as vivid as her own reflection.

"I played along with you," Melanie told them, her voice shrill, trembling. "I played your game. I *helped* you!"

Melanie's knees trembled so hard, she thought she might fall. She gripped the edge of the dresser with both hands.

"Please—" she begged the grinning faces. "I did everything you wanted. But I can't anymore!"

She took a deep, shuddering breath. "Do you hear me?" she shrieked. "Are you listening to me? Why won't you answer me? I can't play anymore! I have to stop! Why can't you understand that?"

Melanie stopped to catch her breath. The shouting caused her throat to ache. Her knees trembled even harder.

She pushed herself away from the dresser. Forced herself to turn away from the eerie faces floating so coldly in the glass.

"I'm l-leaving," she stammered. "You can't stop me. I—I'm not afraid of you two."

She took a shaky step toward her bedroom door. Then another.

She didn't see the long, thin silvery cord stretch out from the mirror glass.

She didn't see the shiny cord as it swung out from the mirror like a whip.

Heart thudding, Melanie started to run.

She ran two or three steps before the silvery cord snapped around her neck—

And sliced her head off.

Sliced it off so neatly, so clean—her body ran another two or three steps before it even realized the head was gone.

Chapter One

Marla Newman loaded her tray and gazed around the lunchroom. Practically every table was filled. With a sigh she dropped her tray down across from Kenny Klein.

"You're having the tacos, too?" she asked, brushing back her wavy red hair and sitting down. "How are they?"

"Not bad," Kenny replied with a mouthful. "Not too rubbery."

"Quite a recommendation," Marla replied, twisting open her bottle of iced tea.

"You'd better eat it all up," Kenny said, grinning his toothy grin. "You're going to need your strength if you plan to beat me in the debate this afternoon."

Marla's throat tightened.

The history class debate. All week Kenny had been trying to make her nervous about it. He'd do anything to gain an advantage.

But she had to win. She had to stay one step ahead of Kenny. Her grade-point average was exactly one-tenth of a point better than his. That one-tenth of a point put her at the top of the senior class.

And Marla was determined to stay there.

After all, what's the point of being second best?

Calm down, she told herself. Don't let Kenny get to you. She gave him a wry smile. "Good luck this afternoon," she murmured.

"Marla—you've already won for best dressed," a girl next to Kenny said. "Great outfit."

Marla flashed the girl a quick smile, then gazed at Kenny's worn jeans and torn white T-shirt. She glanced down at her own pale green silk shirt and ivory wool miniskirt.

Marla spent almost as much time picking out her outfit as she had studying for the debate. She knew she looked terrific—cool and sophisticated.

Her mother always told her that you can spot winners. Because they *look* like winners.

"She's right," Kenny admitted. "You look great."

Kenny is up to something, Marla thought. He never compliments me.

"I think that you're *adorable*, too," she said

sarcastically. "But I'm still going to win." She took a small, delicate bite of her taco.

Kenny pushed a strand of brown hair off his boyish face. "I just wanted to wish you luck," he told her. "Really."

Marla rolled her eyes. "For sure," she said. She finished lunch quickly, her mind ticking off a list of things to do. She had to review her points for the debate one more time. Then she wanted to go over her French homework and—

"Look out!" someone shouted.

Marla cried out as something bumped her arm. As she spun around, she felt something wet and cold splash over her silk blouse.

"Hey—" she cried out angrily.

Clarissa Turner stood beside her, holding her tray awkwardly. Clarissa's iced tea bottle lay on its side on the tray.

Marla's heart sank as she gazed at the large brown stain on her blouse. "Clarissa! I don't believe it!" she shrieked.

A dead silence fell over the cafeteria.

Clarissa shook her head. Her brown eyes were wide with alarm. "I'm sorry, Marla. Really," Clarissa said. "It was an accident."

"Why didn't you look where you were going?" Marla cried, trying to wipe off her shirt with a napkin. "How could anyone be so stupid?"

Clarissa's eyes narrowed. "I *said* I was sorry."

"Sorry won't dry-clean my blouse in time for

7

the debate next period," Marla growled.

"What do you want me to do?" Clarissa asked. "Trade tops with you?"

Marla looked at Clarissa's big plaid flannel shirt. "No, thank you," she said coldly. "This is bad, but *that* would be a disaster."

"You are such a snob!" Clarissa cried. "I didn't mean to spill my drink all over you, but you don't have to go nuts!"

Marla felt a red-hot wave of rage wash through her. She wanted to wipe that smug expression off Clarissa's face.

Clarissa shrugged. "Guess you just won't be Miss Perfect today," she said. "Get used to it, girl, 'cause the truth is, you never really were."

Marla bit her lip and tried to stay calm. She clenched the napkin so tightly, her knuckles turned white. Her head throbbed as she watched Clarissa saunter away.

I wish she'd fall flat on her face, Marla thought, gritting her teeth. Right now!

Clarissa took two steps. Then she screamed as her feet went out from under her.

Marla watched in disbelief as Clarissa toppled facedown. She hit the floor hard.

Marla tried to hold back her laugh, but a little giggle escaped. What an awesome coincidence!

"Hey!" Clarissa shouted. She got to her feet and turned to Marla, her dark eyes blazing. "You pushed me! I can't believe you actually *pushed* me!"

Marla staggered back in shock. "What are you talking about? I didn't move from here. I didn't do anything."

"Give me a break, Marla!" Clarissa cried. "I felt your filthy hands on my back!"

"I didn't touch you!" Marla insisted. "Admit it. You're just a total klutz."

"Yeah, right," Clarissa said. "You need help, Marla. I think you've been studying way too hard. I think you're *sick*!"

"But, Clarissa, really, I didn't . . ." Marla let her voice trail away as the other girl marched off to a table across the room.

Clarissa sat down next to her usual lunch buddies—Josie Maxwell, Jennifer Fear, and Trisha Conrad. Immediately the girls started laughing.

They're laughing at me, Marla realized. I didn't do anything to Clarissa. *She* poured tea on *me*! So why do I feel totally humiliated?

She examined the stain on her blouse. It's not the end of the world, she told herself. All I have to do is focus on the debate and I'll be fine.

Marla glanced at her unfinished lunch and then pushed it away.

"Marla?" an unfamiliar voice asked. "Marla Newman?"

Marla raised her head.

Two girls stood over her. One of them was tall and thin with long, straight blond hair and piercing blue eyes. The other was shorter and fuller, with a frizzy mass of dark curls. Both of them were dressed head to toe in black.

Great, Marla thought. Two members of the Addams Family! "What do you want?" she asked them.

"I'm Roxanne Vale," said the blonde, taking a seat across from Marla.

"And I'm Elena Cross," said the dark one, plopping herself down next to her friend.

"We're juniors," Roxanne added. "Nice to meet you." She extended her hand.

Marla stared at it blankly. Odd jewelry covered the girl's hand. Coiled snakes and bats and skulls glittered across the long, bony fingers.

"What do you want?" Marla repeated.

"Friendship," Roxanne said bluntly, pulling her hand back.

Oh, terrific, Marla thought. They're freaks, they're juniors, *and* they want to be my friends.

"Friendship is power," Elena said to her mysteriously.

Marla rolled her eyes. "You're kidding, right? Why would I be friends with a couple of . . . *juniors*?" She almost said weirdos.

"Because," Roxanne said. "You're one of us."

"One of us!" Elena echoed.

Marla shook her head. "I don't think so," she replied. "I happen to be a senior."

"That doesn't really matter," Roxanne said, a

serious expression on her face.

An uneasy feeling spread down Marla's chest as the blond girl leaned closer from across the table.

Roxanne's icy-blue eyes bore into Marla's. "You have the power," she whispered.

Chapter Two

"What are you talking about?" Marla asked. "What power?" These girls were even wackier than they looked. Roxanne smiled. "I think you know," she replied. "We just saw you push that girl—with your mind."

"*You* are a freak," Marla told Roxanne. "And I was already having a pretty demented day. So why don't you two get lost, okay?"

Roxanne and Elena glanced at each other. Then they turned back to Marla.

"We have the power, too," Roxanne whispered.

"We can show you how to use it," Elena promised.

Marla fought off a sudden urge to scream. "Look," she said through clenched teeth, "the only power you two have is the power to annoy people. Now get *lost!*"

Roxanne and Elena jerked back in their seats. Anger and hurt flashed across their pale faces. Slowly they rose to their feet—and stared coldly at Marla.

Their eyes.

Their eyes were so sharp, so piercing.

"You'll change your mind," Roxanne said. "You'll see."

Marla stood behind a podium on the stage of the darkened auditorium. The first three rows were filled by the two senior honors history classes. She knew they were watching her every move.

Marla glanced down at her blouse. She'd gotten most of the stain out with cold water and paper towels. That wasn't the problem.

The problem was Kenny, standing at the podium on the other side of the stage. He was so calm and confidant, it made her sick.

And he was winning the debate.

"Expansionism," Kenny declared in a strong, steady voice, "is the political result of arrogance and ambition. And ambition has blinded humanity, sparked wars, and spawned murder. Throughout history there have been countless examples. . . ."

On and on Kenny argued his points forcefully. Marla thought this debate on "The Pros and Cons of Ambition as a Historical Force" would be a piece of cake.

After all, what could possibly be *bad* about ambition?

She began to mentally review her arguments, but soon found herself gazing out at the audience.

Mickey Myers and Josh Maxwell sat side by side, cracking jokes to each other, not listening to a word.

Clarissa Turner leaned back in her seat and folded her arms across her chest. Josie Maxwell tugged on Clarissa's sleeve and whispered in her ear. They giggled.

Trisha Conrad and Jennifer Fear leaned forward to join in the fun. They stared up at Marla and snickered.

Forget it, Marla told herself. They're losers. Especially Josie.

Marla didn't exactly know why she hated Josie Maxwell so much. Josie just rubbed her the wrong way. That's why I decided to work in Dad's hardware store over the summer, Marla remembered. Marla's father had originally hired Josie for the job. But then Marla suddenly decided *she* wanted the job instead.

Marla tried to focus on what Kenny was saying, so that she could refute his points. But for once she couldn't. She could barely remember her own arguments.

Concentrate, Marla ordered herself.

14

Her mind drifted again. She remembered the two strange girls at lunch earlier that day—Roxanne and Elena.

What weirdos, Marla thought. The ridiculous black clothes. That freaky jewelry. And all that stupid stuff about *the power.*

Marla shook her head and gazed out across the room. In the darkness two pairs of eyes seemed to gleam brighter than the rest. They beckoned her. Teased her. Dared her to look . . .

Marla gasped as she spotted Roxanne and Elena, standing by the double doors of the auditorium. What are they doing here? she wondered.

A strange coldness tingled in Marla's throat.

Marla tore her eyes away from them. She took a sip of water from the glass on the podium and tried to watch Kenny. Tried to listen to his words . . .

"And what is at the root of most ambition?" Kenny asked the audience. "Selfishness and greed, that's what."

He finished his speech. The auditorium erupted with applause. "Go, Kenny!" Josh shouted out. Mickey whooped.

Mr. Bartleby, one of the history teachers, stood up and stepped to Kenny's podium. The white spotlights gleamed on his bald head. He adjusted his glasses and cleared his throat.

"And now," Mr. Bartleby announced,

"presenting the final counterpoint, is Miss Marla Newman."

Marla could hear a murmur from the audience.

"Quiet, please." Mr. Bartleby turned to her. "Whenever you're ready, Marla."

Marla took another sip of water, set the glass down, and glanced at her notes. Then she started to speak.

But nothing came out.

Marla touched her throat with her hand and swallowed hard. She tried to talk again.

Nothing.

A bead of sweat trickled down Marla's forehead. It's just nerves, she told herself.

She opened her mouth.

A weird gasping sound came from her throat.

Marla felt herself panicking. She was fine earlier in the debate. She rubbed her throat.

What happened to my vocal cords?

Just try harder, she told herself. Try harder!

She took a deep breath and—

"BURRRRRPPP!"

The auditorium exploded with laughter. Marla felt her face grow hot with embarrassment.

"That's classic!" Mickey shouted out.

Marla gazed helplessly across the sea of laughing faces—until she spotted Roxanne and Elena.

They weren't laughing.

Marla's mind reeled—something inside her throat grew thicker. Tighter.

She couldn't talk, she couldn't scream, she couldn't even breathe.

I—I'm choking to death! she realized.

Chapter Three

Marla was still gasping when Mr. Bartleby declared Kenny the winner. The students cheered and jumped to their feet, crowding toward the exit doors.

Marla felt dizzy. The lights and the laughter faded away. A silent scream echoed in her lungs. She needed air.

I'm dying, she thought. Can't breathe . . . Can't breathe!

But no one seemed to notice.

Her eyes fixed on Roxanne and Elena. The two girls in black glided calmly toward the exit. They turned and gazed at her one last time. Then they slipped out the door.

Marla felt the muscles in her throat relax. She took a deep breath. Cool, fresh air filled

18

her lungs. She cleared her throat—her voice was back!

Relief filled her, and she let her head sink into her hands. She was going to be okay.

Kenny came up behind her. He put his hands on her shoulders. "Are you all right, Marla?" he asked.

"Y-Yes, I think so," she said. "I don't know what happened."

Did Roxanne and Elena have something to do with it? Marla wondered. The power?

No. That's stupid, she told herself. Kenny won. He made you nervous and you messed up.

"Let me walk you to our next class." Kenny said, leaning down to grab Marla's backpack. "Hey, better luck next time."

Luck?

Yeah. Kenny was lucky that Marla freaked out and lost her voice. Now she had to face her mother when she got home. Tell her that she lost.

"Look, I don't need your help, okay?" Marla told him, grabbing her backpack from his hands.

"Oh, yeah, I forgot. This school isn't big enough for two valedictorians," he said with a smile. "Even so, you could congratulate me on my victory, right?"

Marla headed for the door. "Some victory! You won by default."

"Yeah, well . . . we'll see who gets a higher grade on the French test," he replied as she left the auditorium.

Marla didn't know what to say. Kenny was great with languages. And French was her worst subject. "Fine." She turned and made her way through the crowded halls.

Marla rounded a corner and spotted Clarissa and Josie. She didn't want to deal with them and tried to slip past.

"That was an *awesome* debate," Clarissa said mockingly.

"Yeah," Josie added. "Too bad you choked up!"

The two girls burst into giggles. Marla hurried down the hall, their laughter ringing in her ears. This day can't get any worse, she thought.

Marla took her seat in Mr. Leroux's French class—the one class that was hard for her.

She could almost hear her mother's voice in her head: "You know, Marla, I never had any trouble with languages. You're probably not studying hard enough."

Is that my problem? Marla wondered. Sometimes she felt as if she did nothing *but* study. Then again, her mother considered anything less than perfection a failure.

Mr. Leroux took out a thick clump of papers. "I know this is the moment you've all been waiting for," he said. "I've graded your exams."

Mr. Leroux slicked back his black hair and stood up. One by one he passed out the graded tests.

Josh breathed a sigh of relief when he saw his score. Phoebe Yamura lowered her head until her long black hair covered her face. Will Reynolds muttered something angrily. And Dana Palmer shook her head in disappointment.

Finally Mr. Leroux reached Kenny and Marla. Marla crossed her fingers and glanced anxiously at Kenny.

"Excellent, Kenny," Mr. Leroux said. He handed the test paper to him. Even from where she was sitting, Marla could see a fat red 97 on the top of the page.

Then Mr. Leroux turned to Marla. "Very good, Marla," he said.

Marla glanced down at her test and studied her grade: 85.

That was a B when she needed an A.

First the debate disaster and now this.

How was she going to explain it to her mother if Kenny turned out to be valedictorian?

"How did you do, Marla?" Kenny asked. He leaned over and sneaked a peek at her test. "Bad break," he said.

Marla shut her eyes. When is this day going to end?

The intercom on the wall crackled, and

Marla opened her eyes.

"Quiet, everyone!" Mr. Leroux snapped. "They must be making a special announcement."

The intercom hissed. Then a voice boomed over the loudspeaker. Mr. Bartleby's voice.

"Quiet, please. . . . Whenever you're ready, Marla."

Marla froze and listened.

No, she thought. *No, it can't be.*

But it was.

A tape recording—of the debate!

Marla held her hands over her ears and tried to block out the sounds. Those terrible, embarrassing sounds . . .

First, a gasp. Then an awful choking noise. Finally the worst sound of all . . .

"BURRRRRPPP!"

Marla felt her face redden. Laughter exploded all around her.

Matty Winger spun around in his seat. "Whoa! A classic moment!"

Marla grabbed her books and jumped up from her desk. Then she raced into the hallway and down the corridor. She could hear the laughter in every classroom she passed. She was the joke of the entire school.

Who? she asked herself. Who would do this to me? Who would tape-record the debate and sneak into the AV room and—

The AV room! she thought. I can catch them in the act!

She turned a corner at full speed—and crashed into Roxanne and Elena. "Out of my way!" she shouted.

The two girls jumped back, their jewelry clanking.

Marla ignored them and forged ahead. At last, she reached the AV studio, a big metal door with a red sign over it. The sign flashed in red: ON THE AIR.

She grabbed the doorknob and pushed. It wouldn't budge. Someone must be blocking it, Marla thought.

With a hard kick she burst the door open.

Inside, a chorus of voices screamed.

"You!" Marla bellowed, gasping for breath. "All of you!"

Josie froze. She stood over the console desk, holding a small tape recorder up to the microphone. Jennifer and Trisha leaned against her shoulders.

Seeing Marla, their faces dropped. Their smiles vanished.

Marla heard a sound behind the door. She pulled it back and stared down at Clarissa, who was crouched down, rubbing her head.

"I should have known," Marla said. "I should have known you losers would be behind this."

The four girls didn't move.

Then Josie stepped forward. "I finally got you back for stealing my job last summer," she said triumphantly. "You thought it was so funny, right? Now look who's laughing. Everybody!"

"The joke's on *you*," Marla said. "All of you! Because I'm the one who's getting out of this nothing town. I'm the one who's going to Harvard or Yale or Brown. And I'm the one who's going to get exactly what I want in life—while you'll all be stuck in Shadyside playing dumb jokes on each other! You'll all be sorry you did this."

Josie rolled her eyes. "Oh, really, Marla?" She smirked. "Nice speech. Is that some sort of threat?"

Marla shook her head. She glanced from one girl to the next: Josie, Trisha, Jennifer, Clarissa. Then she narrowed her eyes.

"It's not a threat," she replied. "It's a promise."

Chapter Four

Marla slammed her French book shut during study hall. Why bother studying? she asked herself. She couldn't get her mind off what had happened that day.

Kenny is going to be valedictorian, and I'm going to be the senior joke. This is so wrong. After four years of hard work . . . It's not fair!

Tossing the book aside, Marla reached for a clean sheet of paper from her backpack. She grabbed a felt-tipped pen and wrote in large block letters across the top:

PEOPLE I HATE.

She smiled.

This, she thought, is going to be fun. Giggling to herself, she started composing her list:

1. KENNY KLEIN (for competing so hard to snatch the valedictorian title away from me—and

then pretending he's my friend).

2. JOSIE MAXWELL (for tape-recording my most embarrassing moment).

3. CLARISSA TURNER (for being a general, obnoxious pain—and spilling iced tea on my best blouse).

4 and 5. JENNIFER FEAR and TRISHA CONRAD (for helping Josie and Clarissa make a fool out of me).

Marla stopped writing and grinned. This was the first time all day she felt good.

She bit the tip of her pen, searching her mind for more names to add to the list.

It was too much fun to stop.

6. MATTY WINGER (for being an annoying geek twenty-four hours a day).

7 and 8. DANA PALMER and PHOEBE YAMURA (for ditching me at Josh's party last week).

9. CLARK DICKSON (for being weird).

On and on Marla kept adding to the list—until half of Shadyside High was on it. Every student who ever bothered her. Every teacher who ever gave her a B. Every coach and janitor and cafeteria lady . . .

The bell rang.

Marla glanced at the list one last time. That was fun, she thought. Good, evil fun. She crumpled it up in a ball. And shoved it into her backpack.

Normally she didn't bother doing petty stuff like that.

But today was far from normal. "Good thing I got that out of my system," she whispered to herself. "Now back to the real world."

Marla let the front door slam behind her. She sighed. It was over. The worst school day in her entire life was finally over!

"Marla, is that you?" her mother called.

Mrs. Newman gasped when she entered the living room. "Marla, honey, what's wrong?" she asked. "You look terrible."

The tall, middle-aged woman rushed to her daughter's side and led her into the living room.

"Here, sit down," Mrs. Newman said softly, lowering Marla into the yellow-flowered sofa. "Now tell me what's wrong."

Marla gazed up at her mother. How can I tell her? she wondered. She'll be so disappointed in me.

"I—" Marla started to speak, then stopped. She couldn't tell her mother that she blew the debate. And blew her French test. That she was no longer Number One in the senior class. A total failure.

"Is it the debate?" her mother asked gently, trying to coax a response out her. "Is that it?"

Marla nodded her head slowly.

Mrs. Newman pinched her thin lips together tightly. "Well, you can't win them all," she said. "I suppose."

Marla sighed and turned her head. Her eyes fell upon a collection of family photos on the wall. She focused on the shots of her mom— receiving her college diploma, her master's degree, her Businesswomen of America Award. She looked so young and pretty.

And successful. Her mother oozed confidence and achievement.

Marla sighed. I bet Mom never had a day like this.

"What about your French test?" Mrs. Newman asked cheerfully. "Did you get your grade back today?"

Marla tried to avoid her mother's inquisitive stare, but she couldn't.

"Let me see it," her mother said softly. "It can't be that bad, now, can it?"

"This whole day rots," Marla groaned.

"Let me see your test," her mother insisted.

Marla knew there was no getting out of it. She reached into her pack for the folded-up test paper. With another unhappy sigh, she handed it to her mother.

She shut her eyes, waiting for her mother to tell her what a disappointment she was. How she wasn't living up to her potential. How a B-plus just announced to the world that she was ordinary and average.

Her mother was silent. Marla opened her eyes.

"Marla, you really are too hard on yourself," her mother said.

Huh? Did Marla hear right?

"A ninety-eight is hardly the end of the world," her mother continued. "You were so upset, I thought you got an eighty or something."

A ninety-eight?

Marla grabbed the test paper from her mother. There at the top of the page was a red 98. Marla gazed hard at the test. It was definitely hers.

What's going on? Marla wondered. I was sure that I got an eighty-five. Maybe with all that happened today I read my paper wrong. Is that possible?

Her mother sat down in the blue wing chair. "I'm very proud of your improvement in French," she told Marla. "Now it's time to work on your debating skills. We still have a little work ahead of us if we want to be valedictorian, right? We can't stop studying just because it's the spring of your senior year."

"Mom, I haven't stopped studying," Marla assured her.

"Do you or don't you want to be valedictorian?" Mrs. Newman demanded.

"I do," Marla mumbled. Why couldn't her mother just ease up for once?

"Then you're going to have to really hit the books," Mrs. Newman told her. "Right now."

"Right now?" Marla groaned. She felt so drained she couldn't imagine doing anything except vegging in front of the TV.

"Yes, right now. The school year is almost over. We don't have much time left."

Marla dragged herself to her feet. She picked up her backpack and headed for the stairs.

I didn't even get a chance to tell her about the rest of my day, she thought. About how everyone was laughing at me.

She climbed the steps slowly, one by one, until she reached her bedroom. Slamming the door behind her, Marla threw herself on the bed. She started to cry but stopped herself.

No tears, she vowed.

She opened her French notebook and pulled out her test. She studied the paper. Definitely a ninety-eight.

"I am so stressed out," she muttered.

Marla woke up the next morning, feeling a little better.

Her heart sank at the thought of going back to school that day. But she had to. She had to show everyone that she was strong. That their teasing didn't bother her a bit.

She was above all that.

After a quick shower Marla dried her hair until it fell in perfect red waves. She put on a touch of makeup, then picked out one of her favorite outfits, a yellow knit dress that clung in all the right places.

Just one last mirror check—she looked

great—and Marla was up and out the door.

The sun sparkled in the sky. Birds chirped, and squirrels dashed from tree to tree. By the time she reached the school, Marla felt ready for anything.

And then she saw Mr. Leroux crossing the school parking lot, heading straight toward her.

Marla pretended not to see him and started in the opposite direction. It's way too early in the morning for Mr. Leroux, she thought.

"Marla!" he called out. "Do you have a minute?"

Marla turned and smiled at him. "Of course, Monsieur Leroux."

"It's about the grade on your test, yesterday," he began.

Marla's heart pounded. The test? Was there some sort of mistake? "The, uh . . . ninety-eight?" she asked hesitantly.

The French teacher nodded. "Yes. I just wanted to congratulate you. Very impressive," he said. "Keep up the good work."

"Uh . . . thanks," Marla said.

She stared at the school building. Maybe today won't be so bad, she thought. Maybe no one will even remember the debate disaster. Maybe I still have a chance to be valedictorian.

Marla took a deep breath and smiled. "I'm back . . . finally!"

She entered the school, holding her head high.

An instant hush fell over the crowded hallway. Everyone turned toward Marla.

Marla froze. "What is everybody staring at?" She glanced down at her outfit. Perfect, she said to herself. What's going on?

And then it began all over again.

The laughter.

But this time the laughter was different. Almost as if there was an anger in the air.

Josie pushed her way through the crowd. She sauntered up to Marla and smirked. "Real mature, Marla," she said flatly. "You're on my hate list, too!" She turned and stormed away.

Marla's heart almost stopped.

Hate list?

Across the lobby a small crowd of students swarmed around a bulletin board.

Marla bit her lip and marched ahead. She pushed her way through the crowd, getting closer and closer to the bulletin board.

She glanced up—and froze.

Pinned to the board was a crumpled sheet of white paper.

Across the top, in Marla's large blocky letters, were the words: PEOPLE I HATE.

Chapter Five

Marla couldn't believe her eyes. The hate list—*her* hate list—hung on the school bulletin board for everyone to see!

How did it get there? she wondered. It was in my bag!

She unzipped her bag and checked for the paper.

Gone.

Now they're all going to hate *me*! she thought in a sudden wave of panic.

Quickly she reached up and snatched the list from the board. Then, stuffing it in her bag, she turned and stomped through a laughing group of students.

Marla's heart pounded in her chest. Spinning around, she took off down the hall. But the laughter followed her.

Reaching her locker, she took a deep breath.

How could this happen? Yesterday I shoved that list in my backpack. *How could this happen?*

Marla felt another wave of panic. Get a grip, she told herself. The school year is almost over. Stay strong. Stick it out.

She opened her locker, deposited her books, and pulled out a blue gym bag. She slammed her locker shut, and jumped.

Clark Dickson stood behind the door.

"Hey—you startled me!" she cried.

He ran a hand through his short black hair and stared at her with his dark eyes. He didn't reply.

Marla always thought he was strange. But now he was giving her the creeps.

"What's your problem, Clark?" she asked impatiently.

Clark fixed a cold eye on her and frowned. "Do you really think I'm weird, Marla?" he questioned her. "So weird that you hate me?"

Marla felt her heart skip. "No, I—I . . . just leave me alone," she stammered, then turned and rushed down the hall. "Everybody—leave me alone!"

"Maybe then you won't hate us anymore!" Matty Winger cried in a high, girlish voice. "Oh, *please*, Marla, don't hate us!"

Ignore them, Marla told herself. After all, I'll be out of here soon.

Marla steeled herself for the long trip to the gym. She knew everyone was mocking her, even hating her. . . .

I'll show them, she told herself. They can't get to me. No matter what they do to me. I'll show them.

She reached the locker room just before the bell rang.

The other girls were already dressed for gym. They leaned against the lockers and straddled the benches in their Shadyside High sweats. They chatted away—until they spotted Marla.

"Oh, look who it is," Trisha said, combing out her long blond hair. "It's the Queen of Hate."

Jennifer slapped Trisha a high-five.

Josie leaned against the lockers and smirked.

She's loving my humiliation too much, Marla thought. I bet she had something to do with this.

Then Marla remembered. Her eighth-period theater class. Josie is in it. She probably pulled the stupid hate list out of my bag when I was working on my scene.

Clarissa crossed her arms over her chest and frowned. "Find anybody new to add to your list, Marla?"

Marla ignored the question. She sat on the bench and started changing, her back to the other girls.

Don't let them get to you, Marla reminded herself.

Mrs. White, the gym teacher, interrupted the scene with a sharp blow of her whistle. "Come on, girls. Move it out."

The girls groaned and headed for the door. Marla sat still on the bench, watching them go.

Then something caught her eye. A glint of silver. The padlock on Josie's locker.

It was unlocked.

Marla waited until the locker room cleared. Then she jumped to her feet. She grabbed Josie's lock and flung open the locker.

Josie's clothes were hanging from a hook— black baggy jeans and a black leotard top.

This is Josie's favorite outfit, Marla thought. She wears it practically every day. Then Marla had an idea.

With a snicker, she gathered up Josie's clothes and headed for the exit.

Peering around the corner, Marla made sure the coast was clear. Then she tiptoed into the empty hall and made a dash for the back door of the school.

This will teach her not to mess with me, Marla thought.

Creeping along the outside wall of the school, she made her way to the cafeteria Dumpsters.

Marla reached up, lifted the heavy metal lid of the Dumpster. The stench was so foul, it made her stomach turn.

Quickly she tossed Josie's clothes into the metal container and let the lid drop.

But she couldn't just go back to the gym. She had to be sure the clothing would be ruined.

Marla held her breath, lifted the heavy lid. Peering into the Dumpster, she spotted Josie's jeans and leotard—resting neatly on top of a cardboard box.

Not good enough.

She had to make sure the clothes were buried deep in the gunk.

Marla reached for Josie's outfit.

Can't reach it. Too far down. She leaned a little farther into the Dumpster—

"Aauugh!"

Marla screamed as she felt someone push her.

Push her hard.

With amazing force.

She toppled into the Dumpster. Her body slid across a gooey mass of rotted vegetables, moldy bread, and curdled milk. She howled in disgust.

Then Marla looked up in horror and screamed again.

"Nooooo!"

The Dumpster lid slammed shut.

Chapter Six

"Ohhhh." Marla uttered a moan of disgust. She pulled herself up from the garbage, the wet, rotting food. Flies buzzed around her ears and face.

Marla gagged.

She reached up to cover her mouth—until she realized her hand was covered with something thick and sticky and putrid smelling.

Her stomach churned.

"I've got to get out of here." Marla tried to stand but slipped and fell.

Bracing her hands on the lid, she pushed as hard as she could.

The lid didn't budge.

"Help!" she shouted. "Somebody!"

Could anyone hear her? She stayed absolutely still, straining to hear if anyone was outside.

She could hear only her rapid breathing and the pounding of her own heart.

And a scratching sound.

A scratching sound?

She felt something skitter across her foot.

Marla let out a bloodcurdling scream. "Let me out!"

The Dumpster lid rattled and opened.

Mickey and Matty stared down at her in shock.

"Is this your new hangout?" Matty joked.

"Please—no stupid jokes. Just help me out of here," she pleaded.

They saw how upset and frightened she was. Her whole body shook. Her stomach lurched again.

Mickey helped lift her out.

She tried to wipe disgusting, clotted clumps of garbage off her skin.

"What happened?" Mickey asked, confused, his face filled with concern. "Did you fall in?"

"What are you doing out here?" Matty asked.

They were trying to be nice, but Marla didn't care. "Bug off!" she muttered, and stormed away.

She yanked open the door to the school.

Josie was standing in the hallway in her gym clothes. "Whoa. Is that a new perfume?" She pinched her nose with her fingers as Marla passed by.

Totally embarrassed, Marla raced to the

locker room. In seconds she peeled off the disgusting gym clothes, and stepped into the shower.

A hot stream of water washed over her. She took a long shower.

Feeling a little better, Marla stepped out of the shower and wrapped a towel around herself. She crossed the locker room and glanced at the clock.

Gym was almost over. She had to get out of there before everyone came back.

"Hello, Marla. We've been looking for you."

Marla spun around.

Roxanne and Elena.

The two girls leaned back against the lockers, casually brushing their hair.

"Well, you found me," Marla said. She turned and headed back toward her locker. She reached for her clothes and started getting dressed.

Elena and Roxanne followed her. "I can't believe the day you're having," Roxanne said. "It stinks that everyone is being so obnoxious to you."

"Yeah, especially that Josie Maxwell," Elena chimed in. "She must really have it in for you."

Marla pulled on her dress and dried her hair with the towel. "I guess," she answered.

"Well?" Roxanne asked, sitting next to Marla. "What are you going to do about it?"

Marla turned and faced the two girls.

"Nothing." She glanced at her smelly gym clothes. "It's not worth it."

Elena broke out in a wide grin. "There's a less painful solution," she said. "A way for you to get exactly what you want."

Marla eyed her suspiciously. "What are you talking about?" she snapped.

"She means your troubles could be over," Roxanne said. "Enemies are easily dealt with."

"Really," Marla said. "And just how do you plan to deal with them?"

"The power," Elena said.

Marla groaned. "Oh, give me a break with this power stuff. It's getting really boring."

Roxanne raised a blond eyebrow. "You don't believe?"

"In what?" Marla demanded. "Magic? Voodoo? Superstitious folk tales?"

"You don't believe in the power?" Elena asked, her eyes wide.

"Well, no. No way," Marla answered truthfully. "That kind of stuff is impossible. It defies the laws of physics, not to mention chemistry and biology."

"What about French?" Elena asked.

"What about it?" Marla asked sharply.

"Your test," Roxanne said. "You got an eighty-five. Until we stepped in. Until we used the power to help you. Now your mother, Mr. Leroux, and even Kenny Klein are convinced that you got a ninety-eight."

Marla felt her jaw drop open. "H-how did you know about all that?" she stammered.

"We called on the power," Roxanne told her. "That's what gave you the A. That's what will give you absolutely anything you want."

"But . . . I thought I really got that A," Marla said. "You guys are joking, right?"

"Straight A's without studying, great clothes, no more bad hair days," Elena said softly. "You can have anything you've ever wanted . . . even valedictorian."

"No. There's no such thing as magic."

That's what Marla had always believed. But inside, she wasn't so sure anymore.

"You can still be number one in your class," Roxanne told her. "Let the power help you, and you'll never have to worry about it again."

Marla couldn't believe that. "Maybe you can change grades on test papers," she admitted. "But there are other factors—like Kenny. He's an excellent student. And he's still ahead of me right now. If we both get hundreds on every test from now until graduation, he'll still be valedictorian."

"Getting him out of the way is simple," Roxanne assured her. "In fact, we can take care of that right away. As soon as you join us."

Elena brushed back a strand of black hair. "Don't you think it would feel good to finally have your mother approve of everything you do?" she asked.

It would, Marla admitted to herself. How did Elena know about her mother and her demands?

How?

"All you have to do is join us," Roxanne said.

Marla sank down onto the locker-room bench. Her head spun. She couldn't imagine that this mysterious power was real. But what if it was?

It would be so great not having to worry about being the best all the time. To be able to relax a little.

Maybe she should give it a try. After all, things couldn't get much worse than they already were.

Marla glanced up at the two strange girls. "Tell me what I have to do."

Chapter Seven

"I knew you'd want to join us." Roxanne sat down beside Marla on the locker-room bench. She looked extremely pleased.

"What exactly am I joining?" Marla asked.

"Think of it as an exclusive club," Elena replied.

"Of what?" Marla asked. "Witches?"

"Not exactly," Roxanne responded quickly. "We like to think of ourselves as . . . students of the Dark Arts."

"The Dark Arts?" Marla echoed.

"Ancient practices . . . as old as the earth itself," Elena said. "It's a long-forgotten science that helps us tap into the power of the earth."

"The power can be used for good or evil. But it's weak if it's used by one person alone. The power reaches its fullest potential when it's harnessed by a circle of three," Roxanne explained.

"That's why we need you, Marla," Elena crooned softly. "You've been blessed with the power, too." She leaned back against a locker and sighed. "We used to have a third member in our circle," she said wistfully. "But then one day she—"

Roxanne glared at Elena, as if telling her to be quiet.

"She had an accident," Elena finished her sentence.

Marla felt a chill tingle up and down her spine. This is all too weird, she thought. Ancient science, secret powers, circles of three.

Maybe I shouldn't do it, Marla thought.

"What do you say, Marla?" Roxanne asked, her voice strained. "Are you ready to join us?"

Marla glanced from one girl to the other. Their eyes sparkled with anticipation. A hunger.

"I—I . . . don't know," Marla stammered.

"Remember," Elena said, "you'll be able to get whatever you want. Anything. Success . . . valedictorian . . ."

"All this without even trying," Roxanne added. "Come on, Marla. It'll be fun. We promise."

Marla turned her head away and gazed up at

the clock. Inside the gym she could hear Mrs. White blowing her whistle. The class would be back in the locker room any second now.

"Okay, I'll do it," Marla said. "Where do I sign up?"

Roxanne grinned. "We'll show you tonight."

"In the Fear Street woods," Elena said. "Midnight."

Marla stopped short when she saw an orange light in the middle of a small grassy field. Her pulse began to race as she heard the sound of chanting.

Roxanne and Elena stood in front of a semicircle of towering candles. They were dressed in flowing black robes. Tall, pointed hoods covered their long hair. Their voices formed a perfect harmony.

As Marla drew closer, she noticed that the candles were black. And in the center of the semicircle of light stood a table covered with a red velvet cloth. A small silver bowl sat on the table.

Roxanne and Elena glanced up. They stopped chanting and smiled.

Marla took a few steps closer and froze. Don't be such a wimp, Marla scolded herself. This is supposed to be fun. "I made it," she announced, a little surprised at the boldness in her voice.

"You're just in time," Roxanne said. "We're

adding the final ingredients to the Summoning Elixir." She nodded at the silver bowl.

Marla leaned over and gazed into the bowl. There was a dark liquid inside. Marla took a sniff. A rancid odor. She pulled back in disgust. "What's it supposed to summon anyway?"

Elena's eyes sparkled. "The Dark Ones," she answered.

Marla swallowed hard.

"You feel scared, Marla?" Roxanne asked. "Don't worry. Nothing bad is going to happen to you."

Marla cleared her throat. "I'm not scared. I'm just cold. Really."

"Here, put this on." Elena offered her a black robe.

Marla took it and slipped it over her head.

"Now we can begin," Roxanne stated in a throaty voice. "Step inside the crescent of candles, Marla. Then the three of us will form a triangle around the altar. Elena, prepare the final ingredients."

The three girls arranged themselves around the small table. Elena held a red satin pouch in front of her. Roxanne closed her eyes and tilted her head back.

Is she going into a trance? Marla wondered.

Roxanne opened her mouth wide. A deep animal growl rose up from her chest, then some strange garbled words.

What language is that? Marla asked herself.

Is it a language?

Her attention was drawn to Elena, who opened the satin pouch, and then dropped the ingredients into the bowl.

A lock of hair. A fingernail clipping. A smooth oval stone. A photograph—though it was too dark for Marla to tell who was in the picture.

The liquid inside the silver bowl began to bubble.

Marla was fascinated. What kind of chemicals are in there? she wondered.

There was no fire near the bowl. And the surface of the liquid was perfectly still before Elena added those four elements.

The liquid bubbled furiously.

"Spirits of the earth. Spirits of the world. Answer my call," Roxanne chanted louder now. "Open the darkness! Open the darkness! Open the darkness!" she cried, singing the words into the night.

The wind howled around them.

The blond girl's voice rose to a shriek. Elena joined her in an animal scream.

This is so weird, Marla thought. She couldn't help it. She found herself completely fascinated by the whole bizarre ceremony.

Marla suddenly trembled. Her whole body shook.

Crossing her arms over her chest, Marla tried to steady herself.

But she couldn't. She couldn't stop shaking.
And soon she realized why.

It wasn't her body shaking.

It was the ground!

Marla searched frantically for a place to take shelter. But the trees swayed wildly back and forth. Rocks and stones rumbled across the ground.

Overwhelmed by panic, she turned to run. Somewhere. Anywhere.

She had to get away.

She staggered a few steps toward the woods.

"Marla! No!" Elena cried.

Marla took another step. The ground swelled up beneath her. She tripped, then quickly pulled herself to her feet.

The earth rose and fell.

"Come back!" Roxanne yelled. "You have to stay inside the crescent!"

Marla ignored her, pushing ahead while trying to keep her balance.

A wide crack ruptured the rocky soil.

Marla screamed.

Then the earth opened up. Opened . . . opened . . .

The crack growing wider—until it swallowed the whole grassy field.

And Marla tumbled down into darkness.

Chapter Eight

Marla plunged into a bottomless pit of swirling blackness.

Falling . . . falling.

I'm going to die, she thought.

I *am* dying!

Then her body jolted to a sudden halt. Something stopped her descent into the chasm.

Marla blinked her eyes and glanced up.

And saw Elena.

The short girl leaned over the side of the pit. Her fingers were held straight out.

Roxanne appeared next to her friend. She peered down at Marla, her blue eyes cold and hard. Then she, too, held her hands straight out.

Together the girls began to chant in some

language Marla didn't recognize.

Marla felt the hairs on the back of her neck stand on end. Slowly but surely she began rising through the air.

"H-How—" she began to ask.

But neither Roxanne nor Elena answered her. They continued to chant, their hands outstretched.

Marla's body tingled as she felt an invisible energy pouring through Elena and Roxanne.

Lifting her higher and higher . . .

They're using the power! she realized. They're using the power to save me!

Marla floated up over the edge of the pit. Higher . . . Higher . . . Finally she collapsed on the ground inside the crescent of candles.

Roxanne and Elena helped her to her feet. "Hurry," Roxanne whispered excitedly. "There's no time to lose. Take our hands and come to edge of the pit."

You've got to be kidding, Marla thought. Back to the edge? No, thanks.

She stared at the bejeweled hands of the two girls. "Look," she said, "I really appreciate you rescuing me, but there's no way I—"

"Come to the edge with us," Elena ordered. "The power is real. I know you felt it. Don't you want to be able to use it for your own good?"

"Yes," Marla said, surprised at her own answer. But it was the truth.

She did want the power.

Marla let them lead her back to the edge of the pit. Sucking in her breath, she gazed down. Beyond the rocky depths.

Into the darkness.

"Repeat after me," Roxanne instructed, squeezing her hand. "I, Marla . . ."

Marla cleared her throat. "I, Marla . . ."

"Summon thee!"

"Summon thee!"

Marla's words echoed in the depths of the pit.

An eerie silence descended upon the woods.

The wind stopped howling.

The trees stopped rustling.

Marla gazed down at a coil of tree roots along the rocky wall of the pit. Slowly a single root began to uncoil, growing longer and longer. The root stretched out from the darkness.

Up, up, up, the tree root extended itself. Until it uncoiled right in front of Marla's face. She clamped her eyes shut and waited for the worst.

But nothing happened.

She opened her eyes. "What's that?"

A single piece of yellowed parchment dangled from the end of the root. It looked ancient. Scrawled from top to bottom in shining black ink, she saw a series of odd, curling letters—a weird language Marla had never seen before.

"It's the pact," Roxanne explained, her eyes glittering.

"Your pact, Marla," Elena said, letting go of Marla's arm. "It will unlock all your powers . . ."

"Once you sign it," Roxanne added.

By the light of the moon Marla studied the parchment. But the letters were completely alien to her except for two familiar words: Marla Newman.

"I can't read it," she said softly.

"It's a lost language," Elena explained.

Marla sighed. "Then how do I know what I'm agreeing to?"

"Sometimes you just have to trust what you know," Roxanne said. "You know that the power gave you that A in French class. And now it just saved you from death."

"If I sign this," Marla asked hesitantly, "what does it mean? What are the terms of the pact? What do I receive?" She gulped. "And what do I give in return?"

"The pact forms your connection to the Dark Forces of the earth," Roxanne replied, pointing into the chasm. "Down there."

Marla gazed into the pit. The darkness stared back. She felt as if it were alive. Like an animal waiting, breathing.

"Wh-What's in there?" she stammered.

"Power," Roxanne told her. "The kind of power that will make you a success at whatever college you get into. That will make you number one in your class at Shadyside before you leave."

Marla thought about it. She'd been so stressed for so long. The idea of just being able to relax a little . . .

"You've only got two months of school left," Roxanne reminded her. "Two months in which you've got to prove that you're the best. In which you can't afford to make one wrong move."

Marla nodded. "Tell me about it."

"And the best part is, the power will make that easy," Roxanne promised her. "You'll have everything you ever dreamed of. Everything you've worked so hard for, Marla. All you have to do is sign the—"

Marla heard a twig snap behind her.

She spun around.

Elena dived toward her.

With a knife.

Chapter Nine

"**N**o! Don't kill me!" Marla screamed. "I'll sign your stupid pact!"

Roxanne burst out laughing. "Don't worry, Marla." She chuckled. "We're not going to kill you. That's not what the knife is for."

Marla sighed with relief. "It isn't?"

"No," Roxanne said. "You're going to cut yourself."

Marla gasped. "What do you mean?"

"For the pact!" Elena explained patiently. "You've got to sign it in blood."

"Your blood," Roxanne added.

Marla gazed down at the knife in Roxanne's hand.

It was big, like a butcher's knife. Its silver handle was covered with an intricate design.

The blade looked sharp and deadly.

"Nothing to it, Marla. It's easy," Roxanne whispered. "This blade is so sharp, you'll barely feel it. It's no worse than a paper cut."

Marla cringed. She hated paper cuts.

"Come on, Marla," Elena urged her. "Just think of all those kids at school. Think about getting back at Josie and Clarissa and Kenny."

"Think of being number one," Roxanne said. "Now and for the rest of your life! Valedictorian is only the beginning."

A flash of lightning crackled through the sky. A strong gust of wind blew through Marla's hair and rustled the leaves in the trees. The eerie sound seemed to dance all around her.

"You're just agreeing to get what you've always wanted," Elena told her.

That's true, Marla realized. I know the power is real. Now I can sign this crazy piece of parchment and use the power. Use it to make the rest of my life go exactly the way I want it to. What am I waiting for?

Marla reached out for the knife. She wrapped the fingers of her right hand tightly around the handle. The steel was surprisingly hot—it burned her skin.

She held out her left palm.

And brought the knife down.

The shiny tip of the blade sliced through her palm in a single, smooth line.

Marla gasped. A tiny stream of dark red

blood trickled across her hand.

I'm going to faint, she thought.

The knife slipped from her hands, its sharp bloody tip stabbing the ground.

Marla blinked her eyes, trying to focus. The woods were spinning now. The trees swirled and danced, round and round her.

She watched Roxanne reach for the ancient parchment. Roxanne broke off the end of the tree root with her long white fingers. Then she held the pact in front of Marla's face.

She grabbed Marla's right arm. She thrust the broken root into Marla's hand.

"Sign it," Roxanne commanded. "In blood."

With a trembling hand, Marla dipped the tip of the root into the blood on her palm.

Roxanne held the pact directly below the dripping red point.

Marla lowered the branch to the bottom of the yellowed parchment.

She hesitated for a moment. Then signed her name on the pact.

Roxanne and Elena shrieked with delight.

"The tree root!" they howled. "Toss the root into the pit!"

Marla followed their orders. She leaned over the edge of the yawning chasm and dropped in the bloodstained root.

Her eyes widened as it fell. Down, down, down . . .

Into the infinite darkness.

The earth rumbled and shook.

Marla teetered forward, losing her balance. Elena grabbed her and pulled her away from the edge.

"Now what?" Marla asked, gasping for breath.

"You'll see," Elena crooned.

The earth trembled. The wind blew faster and harder. The trees rocked back and forth in a frenzy.

And something roared from the depths of the pit.

Marla turned. Out of the dark hole came a strange red light.

She stepped forward to see what it was.

A sudden blast knocked her back.

A powerful burst of flames exploded from the pit.

Marla was showered in sparks. Thick black smoke rose up into the sky, higher and higher. It covered the moon and stained the clouds black.

Marla turned her gaze upward.

Lightning flashed over her head.

Thunder crashed.

Marla screamed in terror. She'd never seen a storm like this before. So powerful. So furious.

A deafening crack of thunder made Marla spin around. High above the trees she glimpsed a jagged bolt of blinding white lightning. She squinted her eyes. The lightning crackled.

It reached down from the sky.
Down to the earth.
Down to Marla.
She covered her face and screamed as the lightning shot over her.

Chapter Ten

Marla sat up in bed with a start.

Sunlight streamed through her bedroom window. The alarm clock buzzed on her nightstand. She reached over and turned it off.

I'm home, she realized. In bed. In my nightshirt.

Rubbing her eyes, she yawned and stretched.

"A dream," she said with a sigh. It was all just a dream. The crescent of candles, the pit, the knife, the pact . . .

The odd thing was she felt vaguely disappointed. It had felt so real. But it wasn't.

With a sigh Marla flopped back on her pillow.

Something crinkled beneath her.

Marla turned—and saw the wrinkled parchment. Strange black letters filled the yellow paper from top to bottom. Black letters surrounding her name.

And at the very bottom of the document, her name again. Her signature—in dried blood.

The pact, she thought. It wasn't a dream!

Her heart started racing.

She raised her left hand and examined her palm. A small scar slashed across the skin. Dark flecks of dried blood stained the wrist.

"I did it," she whispered to herself. "I really did it. I signed the pact!"

A jolt of excitement surged through her body. She felt rested and refreshed, bursting with energy.

She felt *powerful*.

Swinging her feet out of the bed, Marla jumped up and dashed to the mirror above her dresser. She studied her reflection.

Her skin glowed. Her eyes sparkled. Her hair looked thicker, fuller, more lustrous.

She looked terrific.

A wicked smile flashed across Marla's lips.

I did it, she thought gleefully. I joined Roxanne and Elena.

I have the power now.

A short while later Roxanne and Elena were waiting for Marla at her locker at school.

"Good morning, girls!" Marla chirped. "What's up?"

"You look great," Elena said, nodding with approval at Marla's slinky black dress. "How do you feel?"

"Like a brand-new woman," Marla answered. "I'm so energized, I feel like doing something . . . outrageous!"

Roxanne and Elena giggled. "What do you have in mind?" Roxanne asked, raising a blond eyebrow.

"Oh, I don't know," Marla answered. "I was thinking of something sweet, like . . . revenge!"

"The list!" Elena said under her breath. "Do you have your hate list with you?"

"Never leave home without it!" Marla replied. She reached into her bag and pulled out the crumpled piece of notebook paper. She opened it up and read the words: "People I Hate."

"Let's see," Roxanne said. "Who's first?"

The three girls gathered in a tight circle and began going over the list of names.

"There are so many here," Elena murmured. "It's hard to know where to start. I suppose there's always Josie."

"No. Josie is too easy a target," Roxanne declared over the clang of the first-period bell. "We can take care of her later."

"Whoa, slow down!" Marla said. "This is all still new to me. I need a little time to get used to it. Besides, I've got calculus now."

"Then we'll talk later," Roxanne promised.

"Just remember, now you have the power to do *anything* you want."

Marla's day was going great. A ninety-nine on her calculus exam and an A on her English essay. Then the principal called her out of history class to say he was nominating her to be president of the Shadyside High National Honor Society.

The day is going so well, Marla thought on her way to French, I don't even mind that Kenny got a hundred on his calculus exam.

Even though the late bell had rung at least five minutes ago, Marla was humming when she walked into Mr. Leroux's class.

Big deal. So I'm late, she said to herself.

Yesterday, being late for class would have made her frantic. But today she didn't care. She had the power now. She could do anything she wanted.

Mr. Leroux glanced up from his desk. "Mademoiselle Newman," he said, "glad you could join us."

"No problem," Marla said, taking her seat beside Kenny.

"Pas de problème," Mr. Leroux translated her words. Then he turned to Kenny and began speaking fluent French to him.

Marla hated it when Leroux did that. Kenny was the only one who could follow every word when the teacher spoke that fast.

And Mr. Leroux knew it. It was his way of putting down Marla and the rest of the class. Reminding them of how much they didn't know.

Kenny ate it up. He sat there laughing at Leroux's lame jokes and saying things like *"Mais bien sur!"* which meant "But of course!"

The whole act turned Marla's stomach. She wasn't sure who was more obnoxious. Definitely Leroux, she guessed. He was the one who always started it.

She stared at the teacher's thin lips and flashing teeth. Shut up, Leroux, she thought, concentrating on his mouth. Shut up!

Nothing happened.

So much for the power, Marla thought. Maybe I need Roxanne and Elena for this one.

Then Marla's hands grew warm and began tingling.

It's the power, she realized. I can feel it.

Mr. Leroux sputtered.

A white tooth fell from his mouth and landed on his desk.

A few kids gasped. Several others uttered nervous laughter. *"Mon Dieu!"* the startled teacher exclaimed.

Mr. Leroux's eyes widened. And another tooth fell out.

"I—I . . ." Mr. Leroux was no longer speaking French. "I'll be right back!" he said and fled from the room.

It works! Marla thought in amazement. It really works!

Marla leaned back in her seat. A smile played at the corners of her mouth. She had the power now. She could do anything she wanted.

Anything at all.

She gazed at Kenny Klein.

Chapter Eleven

After French class Marla found Roxanne and Elena waiting at her locker again. Both of them were smiling.

"So you took care of Mr. Leroux," Elena said.

"I heard it was totally disturbing!" Roxanne exclaimed, laughing.

Marla shook her head. "I couldn't believe it at first. And poor Mr. Leroux never had a clue."

Roxanne's expression became serious. "So you see how the power works," she said softly.

Marla nodded. "It was awesome."

"And you've only just begun," Elena reminded her. "That was just a sample of what's possible."

"So, Marla," Roxanne said. "Who's next?"

"What do you mean?" Marla asked.

"From the your hate list," Roxanne reminded her. "Who's going to be next to feel your power?"

Clarissa Turner, Jennifer Fear, and Trisha Conrad walked past them, chatting, acting as if Marla weren't standing there.

"Three of your favorite people, right?" Elena whispered.

"You could take care of all three at once. They helped Josie with the public announcement, didn't they?"

Marla narrowed her eyes and nodded slowly. "Yeah. But I don't want to rush. I want to plan something perfect for each one of them."

Clarissa turned around. "Oh, Marla!" she called out. "Did you hear Trisha's good news?"

"What's that?" Marla asked.

Jennifer took a thick white envelope from Trisha's hand and waved it. "She just got into her first choice—Brown! Didn't *you* apply to Brown, too?"

"You . . . you heard from them already?" Marla asked. She couldn't believe it. Her mother called the Brown admissions office a few days ago. She was told it would be another two weeks before letters were sent out.

"Well, my dad has a friend on the board of admissions who pulled a few strings," Trisha admitted.

"Meaning what?" Marla asked. Trisha doesn't have the grades to get into Brown University,

Marla thought bitterly.

Trisha shrugged. "Daddy's going to donate a new student union to the campus."

Marla's jaw dropped. *Trisha Conrad* got into Brown because her father's giving the college a lot of money? That wasn't fair! No way!

"You could at least congratulate her!" Jennifer scolded Marla.

"Congratulations," Marla said between her teeth.

She watched as Trisha and her friends continued down the hall. They were telling everyone the good news. Trisha kept squealing with delight and hugging people.

"That girl has never had to work for a thing," Marla said. "Everything she wants, Daddy hands to her on a silver platter."

"Maybe it's time her luck changed," Elena suggested.

Marla concentrated on Trisha. Trisha was wearing one of her designer outfits. A perfect little miniskirt and a tight lacy top.

"You have to do something," Roxanne whispered.

"I guess I do," Marla agreed.

"Do you want us to join our power to yours?" Elena asked.

Marla shook her head. "No, I can handle this one on my own."

She waited patiently. Summoning the power. Feeling it move through her body. Tingling through her hands.

She concentrated on Trisha. I want to teach you a lesson, she thought. Embarrass you the way you embarrassed me.

Trisha opened her locker, then stooped down to grab her gym bag from the bottom.

Just as Trisha bent down Marla released the power.

Riiiiip.

Trisha's tiny little skirt ripped neatly down the back. It fell to the floor in two perfect halves.

Trisha screamed and tried to cover up. She was wearing really dopey-looking underpants with little blue bears on them.

Marla laughed till her side hurt. Beside her, Roxanne and Elena laughed just as hard.

"That was excellent!" Elena gasped.

"I knew you were going to be good at this!" Roxanne agreed.

The *best*! Marla thought with a tight smile.

"So who's next?" Elena asked. "Come on. Who's next?"

"It's got to be Josie," Roxanne said. "We can't miss this chance. Look, she's heading for the glass doors in the front of the school."

"What does that have to do with anything?" Marla asked.

Roxanne rolled her eyes and dragged Marla toward Josie. "You'll see."

Marla squinted at the sunlight beaming through the big glass doors of the school.

"Let's go outside," Roxanne said. "I'll show you what I mean."

The three girls hurried past Josie and made their way outside. "Josie looked upset," Marla pointed out.

"She's going to look a lot worse," Elena promised with a giggle.

"It's payback time," Roxanne said in a low, mischievous voice. "Josie is almost to the door. All you have to do is push her through it—with the power."

Marla's heart skipped a beat. "But—" she started to protest.

"But what?" Roxanne shot back. "Josie's a creep. She tape-recorded your debate. She played it over the loudspeaker for the whole school. And she's probably planning a repeat performance for graduation!"

"You've got to get her back, Marla," Elena added. "Before she gets *you*."

A sickening wave of terror rushed through Marla's body.

"B-but—push her through a glass door?" she stammered. "That's . . . dangerous."

Elena shrugged. "So is crossing the street."

"It's cruel!" Marla cried.

"True," Roxanne agreed.

"It . . . it . . ." Marla fumbled for the words. "It could kill her!"

Roxanne and Elena stared back at her blankly.

"So what?" they asked.

Chapter Twelve

So what? The words rang in Marla's mind. *So what?*

So what if we kill Josie?

"You can't be serious," Marla choked out, her voice catching in her throat.

Roxanne shrugged. "You don't want her wrecking your graduation speech, do you?"

"Well, no, but—" Marla sputtered.

"But what?"

"I don't want to . . . to . . ." Marla lowered her voice to a whisper. "I don't want to kill her!"

"No?" Roxanne asked, raising her eyebrow.

"Well, we have to do *something* to her," Elena insisted. "We have to stop her."

Marla gazed over at Josie, leaning in the doorway of the school. She turned back to Roxanne and Elena. "We'll get her," she stated firmly. "But let's think of something else. I'll meet you here after school. We'll come up with a new plan."

Roxanne sighed. "If you insist."

"Okay, I'm going to my next class," Marla said, turning toward the school. "I'll see you later."

"Later, Marla," the two girls called.

Marla heard the bell ring for the next period and headed toward the front door. Her feet felt like lead weights. Her head throbbed.

Josie glared at her as she approached. "Hi, Marla," she called. "Steal anyone else's clothes today?"

Marla could feel Josie's hateful stare as she pulled the glass door open and stepped inside. She ignored Josie's bitter question and hurried down the hall.

I just saved your life, Josie, she thought. You could be a little grateful.

Making her way to class, Marla started to tremble. Her mind spun from the shock of everything that had happened.

Signing the pact.

Using the power on Mr. Leroux.

And on Trisha.

And now . . . killing Josie?

That's *insane*! We can't, she told herself. We won't. I'm not a murderer. Roxanne and Elena aren't murderers. *Are* they?

A chill swept down her back. She shook it off.

Look on the bright side, Marla thought. You have the power. You feel terrific. And you look terrific, too.

Marla felt a sudden urge to check herself out again. She ducked into the girls' bathroom.

She leaned over the bathroom sink and studied her face in the mirror. Her cheeks glowed with color. Her shining red hair fell down to her shoulders in thick wavy curls. And her eyes . . .

Her eyes looked different somehow. Darker. Sharper.

Marla pulled away from the mirror.

Yes, there was definitely something new in her eyes.

Something wicked.

Her hands began to tingle.

That's strange, she thought. I'm not using the power now.

But she couldn't deny it—her hands were tingling!

A loud cry made her jump. A long, woeful shriek. From somewhere outside the school.

What's that? Marla wondered.

Then she recognized it. A siren. An ambulance siren?

Marla turned and hurried out of the rest room. She stumbled out into the hallway.

Her hands were still tingling.

Students filled the hall. Scrambling toward the lobby.

"What happened?" Marla called out.

"An accident!" someone yelled. "In the lobby!"

Marla's stomach clenched into a tight ball.

No, it can't be, she thought.

Trapped in the crowd, Marla tried to push her way through the stampeding students. Their nervous voices rose up over the wail of the siren.

"Who is it?" Marla shouted.

"I don't know, but someone said she's hurt really bad!" a boy replied.

Who? Who?

She had to see. She had to find out.

She had to make sure it wasn't . . .

Marla gasped when she saw the front door of the school.

Shattered. Shattered as if a tornado had blown through it. Broken glass littered the floor.

The sirens wailed in Marla's ears. The sound seemed to hypnotize her, luring her forward as if she were in a trance. Step by step, she moved closer. Shards of glass scraped beneath her shoes.

Then she saw a long white stretcher—with a body on it.

Josie Maxwell's body.

Covered in blood.

Chapter Thirteen

"**J**osie!" Marla staggered back, trembling in horror.

And bumped into Roxanne and Elena.

"Hello, Marla," Roxanne crooned in her ear. "So how does it feel . . . to have blood on your hands?"

Marla spun around. "What are you talking about?" she demanded. "I didn't have anything to do with this!"

"Oh?" Roxanne said, lowering her voice to a whisper. "Then why are your hands tingling?"

Marla froze. Roxanne was right. Her hands *were* still tingling!

She groaned and turned back toward the ambulance. White-uniformed medics swarmed around the stretcher, blocking Marla's view.

But she could see the blood. The blood

75

smearing the shards of broken glass.

"No!" Marla whimpered, falling back against Roxanne and Elena. "Is she really . . . dead?" she asked, afraid to hear the answer.

Roxanne and Elena shrugged.

"I've got to know," Marla insisted. She took a couple shaky steps closer to the stretcher.

She gazed down at Josie. Splinters of glass covered the girl's arms and legs and face. She was drenched in blood.

But she was breathing.

She's alive! Marla thought. "Don't die, Josie! Please, don't die!"

Josie shifted and groaned on the stretcher. Her eyes fluttered open. She started to speak.

"I—I didn't walk through the door," she moaned, her voice thin and weak. "I felt a hand pushing me. But . . . but there wasn't anybody there."

The medics tried to get her to stop talking. But Josie wouldn't be silenced.

"Maybe it was the evil spirit," Josie murmured. "The evil spirit from the Doom Spell . . ."

"Huh? Evil spirit?" Marla shook her head. Josie is out of her mind. Talking crazy. She must be in shock.

But Marla knew the truth. Her hands were no longer tingling. But she knew that the power had sent Josie flying through the door.

Marla began to shake uncontrollably.

She had signed a pact. A pact with the Dark Forces. A pact she didn't really understand.

What was I thinking? Marla asked herself. She glanced at Roxanne and Elena. They used my power without me. To really hurt someone.

They might do it again. And who will they hurt the next time? Who will they kill?

Marla shuddered. I have to get out of this! I have to break the pact!

She watched the medics lift Josie's stretcher and roll it gently into the ambulance. Then, with lights flashing and sirens blaring, the ambulance took off down Park Drive.

"Hang in there, Josie," Marla muttered as the sirens faded in the distance.

She knew what she had to do now.

She had leave the circle of three.

She turned to face Roxanne and Elena.

They were gone.

Frantically Marla scanned the area with her eyes. She gazed at the shocked faces of the other students. The two girls were nowhere to be seen.

She turned to the parking lot—and spotted them.

Marla charged after them. "Roxanne, Elena! Wait up!" she called.

The two girls turned around. They waited patiently for Marla to catch up. "Well?" Roxanne asked. "Wasn't that fun?"

Marla was too stunned to answer.

"Bet you didn't know we could use your power without you!" Elena said. Her eyes flashed with amusement.

Marla fell back and leaned against a parked car. She shook her head. "What do you mean? How could you use my power?"

"Your hatred for Josie," Roxanne explained. "Your hatred feeds and strengthens the Dark Forces. We simply tapped into it."

Marla's head spun.

"You should've seen Josie smash through that glass door!" Elena snickered.

"Supergirl! She thought she could fly!" Both girls burst into cold laughter.

Marla felt sick.

It was all a big joke to them!

"I can't do this anymore," Marla managed to utter.

Roxanne and Elena stopped laughing. They stared at Marla sharply.

"What do you mean you *can't*?" Elena asked.

Marla sucked in her breath. "I don't want to hurt people," she said in a trembling voice. "I don't want any part of it."

Roxanne crossed her arms over her chest and narrowed her eyes. "What are you saying, Marla?"

Marla felt a cold wave of fear wash over her. Her hands shook. She slipped them behind her back and tried to gather her courage.

She had to tell them. She had to speak up for herself.

She had to end this nightmare.

"I don't want to be involved in this anymore," she said. "I'm finished. I quit the circle."

"You quit?" Roxanne echoed.

"Yes, I quit," Marla repeated. "I don't want the power anymore. I'm not helping you hurt anyone else."

The two girls stared at her in shock.

"You can't quit, Marla," Roxanne said calmly.

"Why not?"

"You signed the pact," Elena explained. "Don't you get it? You joined our circle. You accepted the power of the Dark Forces."

"We're in this together now," Roxanne told her.

"I can quit if I want to," Marla protested angrily. "You can't *force* me to be part of your little coven."

Roxanne and Elena shook their heads.

"You signed the pact." Roxanne said softly. "In blood. We didn't *force* you. You signed it."

"But . . . but. . ." Marla's heart pounded. Her mind reeled as she stared at their hard, cold expressions. "How long . . . ? How long does the pact last?"

Roxanne smiled darkly. "Forever," she said.

Chapter Fourteen

"It can't be true!" Marla cried. "There has to be a way to break the pact."

She spun around and ran from the parking lot. "I won't do it. I won't stay in the circle!" Marla cried over her shoulder. "I quit!"

Roxanne and Elena called after her.

But Marla didn't care. She had to get away. Away from the blood and the shattered glass.

Away from the evil.

She glanced down at her hands and remembered Roxanne's horrible question—*How does it feel, Marla, to have blood on your hands?*

As she ran, Marla was barely aware of the streets or the traffic. She ran until she reached her house.

She felt numb and sick. And she couldn't imagine that she would ever feel better.

Marla let herself into the house quietly. But her mother heard her.

"Marla?" Mrs. Newman's voice rang out from her office next to the stairs. "Is that you?"

Marla took a deep breath. She stepped timidly to her mother's office door and peered inside. "It's me, all right," she replied breathlessly.

"You're home early, aren't you?" her mother said. "What's wrong?"

"I felt sick," Marla explained. "So I left school."

Mrs. Newman looked up from her desk. She was adding up receipts with a calculator. "Sick? Is it a cold?" she asked, concerned.

Marla shook her head. "I think it's my stomach," she said, making a face. She glanced down at the floor. Her whole body shook.

Her mother frowned. "You'd better go upstairs and lie down. Should I call Dr. Felder?"

Marla muttered no. She turned and climbed the stairs to her room.

She closed the door gently behind her. And locked it.

What am I going to do? she wondered, sitting on the edge of her bed. How am I going to get out of this?

She stood and crossed the room to her desk, opened the bottom drawer, and pulled out the pact. Her eyes scanned the ancient-looking parchment.

There's got to be a way to break this, she

thought. If only I could read what it says.

She gazed numbly at the weird writing. Then, tossing the pact on her pillow, she flopped back onto her bed.

"Forever," she whispered to herself, staring at the ceiling. "They said the pact was forever."

She closed her eyes and pictured the cold, laughing faces of Roxanne and Elena. She shook off the image, opened her eyes again.

And gasped.

Marla gaped in horror as thick, curving black letters appeared on her ceiling. Writing their way from one side to the other, until the entire ceiling was covered.

Marla sat up in bed. Her eyes widened with fear. She turned her head from side to side. The writing covered all four walls.

She recognized the strange, ancient words. They were the words of the pact.

This isn't real, she told herself and rubbed her eyes.

But the vision did not disappear.

The thick, black ink changed color before Marla's eyes. Changed to a crimson red, then dripped from the white walls.

Dripped like blood.

The Dark Forces, Marla thought. They're giving me a sign. They're telling me I can't break the pact.

Jumping up, Marla threw herself at one of the walls. She pounded the words with her fist.

She clawed at the red ink with her fingernails.

"Leave me alone!" she wailed. "I quit! I quit!"

Marla slumped down to the carpet, sobbing. Feeling a twinge as her left hand began to throb. "The pact. Why did I sign it? Why?"

Her face slid across the stained wall. Her skin started burning, and Marla pulled away in pain.

The lines of writing suddenly burst into flames.

Fire and sparks spewed from the walls and the ceiling. The ancient words crackled and burned. Thick, black smoke filled the room.

Marla gagged and coughed. Gasping for breath, she stumbled to the window and flung it open.

Just breathe, Marla told herself. She leaned over the window sill, gasping for air.

This can't be real. Please, let it not be real!

The crackling sound of the fire stopped, and Marla meekly glanced back into her room.

No bloodstained walls. No fiery letters. Nothing.

Her room was back to normal.

Relief flooded her as she pulled herself in from the window. "It's over," she whispered and sank down on the carpet once again. She caught sight of the yellowed parchment resting on the pillow of her bed. "For now."

Marla's hand continued to throb. She gazed down at her left palm and stared bitterly at the pale red wound.

The place where she had cut herself to join the circle of three.

Scars heal, she thought. But the pact lasts forever.

Forever.

Marla threw her head down in despair. Guilt and terror stabbed her conscience.

The strange pulsing in her hand intensified. Cautiously she raised her head and stared again at her aching palm.

Frozen in terror, Marla watched as the skin around the pale wound slowly split open. As if the scar were being cut with a sharp knife all over again.

Marla screamed as the hot blood poured across her hand.

Chapter Fifteen

Exhausted, Marla sat quietly in Mr. Leroux's class the next day. She couldn't sleep at all the night before.

Marla rested her head on her desk as the rest of the class chatted excitedly. Is Mr. Leroux coming in today? she wondered—after what I did to him?

"Bonjour, class," a woman said, entering the room. "My name is Ms. Claire."

A substitute teacher.

Marla stared at the pretty woman and felt a pang of guilt. Mr. Leroux is out because of me.

No matter how hard she tried, the substitute could not control the rowdy French class.

Mickey and Matty, among others, took full advantage of the young teacher's lack of experience, calling out jokes, tossing a tennis ball back and forth every time she turned her back.

"Please! Quiet, please!" Ms. Claire shouted above the noise. "Let's get back to the lesson! We're discussing future tense verbs."

Most of the students ignored her. They passed notes and joked around.

"Mr. Leroux said—" The substitute teacher was forced to yell. "Mr. Leroux said—!"

The mention of Mr. Leroux's name silenced the class.

"How is Mr. Leroux?" Kenny asked the teacher.

Ms. Claire adjusted her glasses and sighed. "I was told by the principal that he's having dental surgery today," she announced patiently. "But if all goes well, he should be back in time for finals."

Finals! Marla remembered in a panic. They're only a couple of weeks away!

She glanced at Kenny Klein. He seemed cool and calm. Totally self-confident.

Well of course, she thought bitterly. He's probably studying every night—while I'm out in the woods signing strange blood pacts.

"Mr. Leroux said you need to work on the future tense," Ms. Claire continued.

The end-of-period bell rang, and everyone jumped up from their seats, laughing and talking.

"Remember, class!" Ms. Claire shouted. "The

future tense will be on your final exam. It's no joke. You'd better start studying!"

Marla moaned to herself as she gathered up her books.

"So how's it going, Marla?" Kenny asked her. "Getting ready for finals?"

Marla shrugged. "I'm not worried about it," she answered as casually as she could. She gave Kenny a forced smile and fingered the new scab on her palm.

Kenny followed her out of the classroom. "If you need any help with your French, I'd be glad to give you a hand," he offered with a smile.

"Thanks, Kenny. I think I'll be okay. But if *you* need any help . . ."

Kenny grinned and started to hurry away.

Marla called out to him. "Kenny!"

He turned around.

Marla lowered her voice. "If you're serious, maybe I'll take you up on your offer," she told him. "Lately I've been too stressed out to study. I could use the help in French. Thanks."

Kenny stared at her, startled. He studied her cautiously.

"I—I mean it," Marla stammered.

She turned toward her next class—and bumped right into Clarissa Turner.

The dark-haired girl spun around. Anger flared in her eyes when she saw Marla.

"I'm sorry, Clarissa," Marla said. "But I'm

glad I ran into you. I wanted to ask you about Josie. How's she doing?"

Clarissa rolled her eyes. "As if you care!"

"No, I do!" Marla insisted. "It was a terrible accident. I wouldn't wish that on anybody!"

Clarissa relaxed a little. "Well, the doctor says she's going to be okay," she explained. "She had a lot of cuts, but they were all minor. She'll probably be back in school next week."

Marla sighed with relief. "If you see her, tell her I hope she gets well soon."

Marla turned and headed down the hall. When she reached her locker, she groaned. Roxanne and Elena were waiting for her.

"We really need to talk to you," Roxanne announced.

The two girls each grabbed one of Marla's arms and led her into an empty classroom. At first Marla tried to protest, but then she went calmly. She knew that she couldn't fight them.

"So, have you changed your mind about the pact?" Roxanne asked, closing the door behind her.

Marla lowered her head, remembering the horror in her bedroom. "I guess I have no choice," she answered unhappily. "But I made a mistake when I signed that pact. A big mistake."

"Don't look back," Elena replied. "You're one of us. You'll learn to enjoy it."

"You've become part of the Dark Forces,"

Roxanne added. "Which means you have to do what the Dark Ones want."

Marla sighed.

Be strong, she reminded herself. Don't let these two intimidate you.

"What exactly do the Dark Ones want?" Marla asked, trying to sound as if she wasn't terrified.

"Blood," Roxanne replied coldly.

"Excuse me?"

"Blood for blood," Elena said.

Marla felt her courage fading. Her stomach tightened.

"You received the power . . . in blood," Roxanne reminded her. "So you must pay back . . . in blood."

Marla glanced nervously across the empty classroom. All the desks and chairs began to spin.

"Blood is the life!" Roxanne shrieked.

"Blood is the power!" Elena cried out.

"Blood feeds the earth!" they chanted in unison. "Blood is the nourishment of the Dark Ones!"

Marla staggered back in horror. Her back struck the chalkboard. "What you are telling me?" she whispered, her voice trembling.

The desks and chairs stopped spinning. Roxanne and Elena gazed coldly at Marla.

"It's simple," Roxanne told her. "As payment for your power, someone must die."

"You're crazy!" Marla protested.

"You signed an agreement," Elena replied.

"Which I couldn't even read!" Marla reminded her.

"Then let me explain the basics," Roxanne said. "If you don't kill someone by the next full moon, then you'll have to die yourself."

Marla couldn't speak.

No! I can't! I can't kill anybody!

"You can do it, Marla," Roxanne assured her. "You know you want to be valedictorian. So here's the one little thing you have to do to get it."

Elena sat casually on a desk. "Come on, Marla," she said. "No big deal. You've always been ambitious. All you have to is kill the one person who stands in your way."

Marla glanced up, confused and afraid. No big deal? *No big deal?*

"What are you *saying*?" Marla cried.

Roxanne smiled—and answered Marla's question.

"You have to kill Kenny Klein."

Chapter Sixteen

Marla stared at Roxanne and Elena in disbelief. "I can't believe you're saying that."

"Why is it such a big deal?" Roxanne asked innocently.

"He's number one on your hate list," Elena pointed out.

It's true, Marla thought. Kenny and I have been rivals since elementary school. I've worked so hard to beat him. For so many years now.

And when I thought he might become valedictorian instead of me, I was ready to do anything.

But kill him?

"No way," Marla said. "I refuse to kill him. I refuse to kill anybody. Do you understand?"

"Marla—" Elena started.

"I'm not going to change my mind," Marla told her. "End of discussion."

Roxanne and Elena exchanged a glance. Then they backed away from her, heading for the door.

Is that it? Marla wondered. Is that all I had to say to get out of this? No. It can't be that easy.

"Where are you going?" she asked them.

"Nowhere," Roxanne answered. "Just stay away from us, okay?"

Marla was confused. They seem almost afraid of me now, she noticed.

Elena frowned and bit her bottom lip. "Come on, Roxanne. Let's get out of here before it's too late."

"What's your problem?" Marla asked her.

Roxanne shot a worried glance at Elena.

"We . . . we don't want to be near you," Elena explained hesitantly. "It's too dangerous."

"What do you mean?" Marla asked.

"We told you," Roxanne said. "If you don't kill for the Dark Forces . . . the Dark Forces will kill you!"

"We don't know how it will happen," Elena added. "Or when it will happen."

"But it definitely *will* happen," Roxanne said. "Unless you kill someone first."

"And we don't want to be around when it comes," Elena said.

The two girls rushed for the classroom door.

Roxanne grabbed the doorknob.

They really seem scared, Marla thought. Is this a big act? Could they be telling the truth?

"Wait!" she shouted to them. "Before you go . . . tell me how you know about this!"

Elena glanced anxiously at Roxanne, then answered Marla's question. "It happened to Melanie," she whispered.

"Melanie? Who's Melanie?" Marla demanded.

"She was a junior. The third member of our circle," Roxanne replied. "She—she refused to kill."

"And what happened to her?"

Elena hesitated. "It was horrible," she whispered. Her eyes seemed far away—as if she were remembering something. "Blood. So much blood . . . everywhere. Poor Melanie."

Roxanne pushed her friend out the door. She turned back to Marla. "We never did find Melanie's head," she said.

Mrs. White, the gym teacher, blew her whistle so loudly, Marla jumped.

She couldn't stop thinking about what Roxanne and Elena had said.

Will the Dark Forces really come after me?

"Line up, girls!" the teacher bellowed like a drill sergeant. "Give me fifty jumping jacks! Ready, go!"

Trisha, Clarissa, and Jennifer crowded into the back row—knocking Marla off balance.

Marla stumbled and caught herself. She shot her classmates a dirty look. Then she sighed and stepped up to the front row.

Just ignore them, she told herself.

"Come on, Marla!" Mrs. White snapped. "Get moving! One! And two! And one! And two!"

Marla pumped her arms up and down, her feet jumping to the rhythm. Her heart started beating fast. Too fast.

What's wrong with me? Marla wondered.

A wrenching pain ripped into the pit of her stomach.

It felt as if her insides were being torn apart.

Marla groaned and doubled over in pain.

Mrs. White glared at her. "It's just a cramp, Marla," the gym teacher grunted. "Work it off. One! And two!"

Marla tried to straighten up. The pain eased a little. And then disappeared. Taking a deep breath, she resumed her jumping jacks.

But the pain stabbed her again.

And again.

Every time that Marla lifted her arms, an invisible knife seemed to plunge into the pit of her stomach.

Mrs. White blew her whistle.

Marla went limp. Gasping for breath, she clutched her stomach.

No more pain.

A wave of fear rushed through her.

Maybe it's the Dark Forces coming to kill me.

Marla stared across the huge gymnasium. Equipment was arranged on the wooden floor. The parallel bars, the trampoline, the balance beam, the chin-up bar, the climbing rope . . .

Marla shivered. Was this it? Was this how the Dark Forces were going to get her? Would they make it look like an accident?

Mrs. White divided the girls into small groups. "Now get to your stations and start practicing!" she instructed.

Marla hesitated.

"Let's go, Marla," the gym teacher urged. "I want to see if you can beat your record time for climbing the rope."

Marla's stomach flopped. Taking a deep breath, she approached the long, knotted rope suspended from the ceiling.

She stepped gingerly onto the crash mat and stared upward. It's so high, Marla thought. If I fall . . .

"Okay, Marla," Mrs. White said, holding up her stopwatch. "I'm timing you. Are you ready? Set?"

Marla grasped the rope with both hands. Her heart raced again.

"Go!" the gym teacher cried.

Marla hoisted herself up, hand over hand. She gripped the rope with her legs, coiling it around her left ankle and bracing it with her right foot. Her hands reached higher.

Beads of sweat formed on Marla's forehead.

She was too afraid to look down. Higher . . . higher. The rope swaying beneath her.

"That's it, Marla!" Mrs. White shouted. "You're making good time. You're doing great!"

Marla's head began to spin. Her heart pounded harder. She could barely breathe.

Keep going, she told herself. Don't look down.

She closed her eyes and climbed. She was almost to the top when she felt the rope wriggle in her hands.

It suddenly felt warm and slick.

It writhed and curled. Like a snake.

A snake?

Marla opened her eyes.

It *was* a snake!

A thick green snake, its scales warm and glistening.

"Ohhhhhh." A terrified moan escaped from Marla's throat.

She heard a hissing sound over her head.

She looked up.

And stared into the eyes of a monstrous cobra. Its giant head rippled and flared above her. A long forked tongue darted out between two pointed white fangs.

The hissing stopped.

The snake fixed its slitted eyes on Marla.

The tongue lashed out. The fangs snapped.

Marla screamed. Lost her grip.

And fell to the gym floor below.

Chapter Seventeen

Marla opened her eyes. A blur . . . A white blur.

She struggled to focus.

She stared up at harsh fluorescent lights on the ceiling. Where am I? she wondered.

Then the posters on the wall came into view—detailed drawings of skeletons, pictures of the muscular system, cross-sections of hearts and lungs and intestines.

The nurse's office, Marla realized.

She tried to lift her head. A sharp jolt of pain surged through her shoulder and neck.

"Ouch!"

The nurse, Ms. Kramer, glanced up from her desk. "Marla?" she said, jumping to her feet. "You're awake!"

The young woman walked over to the examining table. Her crisp white uniform rustled as she approached. "You shouldn't try to move yet," she told Marla gently.

She pushed her wire-framed glasses up her slender nose and stared down at Marla. Aiming a bright light into each of Marla's eyes, she examined the girl's pupils.

Marla gazed back into the nurse's eyes. They were so big and blue and comforting. They made Marla feel safe and secure.

"How am I doing?" Marla asked.

Ms. Kramer snapped off her light and smiled. "Well, you don't seem to have a concussion," she answered. "No internal bleeding. But you're a little banged and bruised."

Marla sighed with relief.

"I guess the crash mat broke my fall," she whispered.

The school nurse nodded. "You're very lucky," she explained. "A fall like that could have caused serious injury. I remember a student who—"

Ms. Kramer stopped talking. She squinted her eyes and leaned forward. She examined Marla's throat.

"That's odd," she mumbled to herself.

"What?" Marla asked, her voice shaking. "What's wrong?"

The nurse didn't answer at first. She aimed her little light on Marla's neck and touched the skin with her fingers.

"What is it?" Marla asked again.

Ms. Kramer shook her head. "I'm not sure," she muttered. "Maybe you scratched yourself when you fell," she suggested, turning toward a cabinet on the wall. "Don't worry. I'll patch you up."

"There are scratches on my neck?" Marla asked.

"Just two," the nurse replied.

Were they scratches? Marla wondered. Or were they fang marks from a creature sent by the Dark Forces?

She remembered how the words of the pact appeared all over her room. How they turned blood-red and then burst into flames. How the scar on her wrist re-opened.

All when she wanted to quit the circle of three. To break the pact.

And now the hideous snake.

Maybe I really am going to die unless I kill Kenny, she thought. But can I really do it? Murder someone?

Marla shook her head. No. Of course not. Of course I can't. A gust of wind rattled the window of the nurse's office.

The Dark Forces are everywhere, she realized. Even here in this room. I can feel it.

An icy chill rushed up Marla's spine. She tried to distract herself by watching Ms. Kramer pull gauze, tape, and scissors from the cabinet.

Just concentrate on something else, Marla told herself.

"Okay, let's get some disinfectant on those cuts," the nurse said.

Ms. Kramer dabbed at Marla's neck with a cold, damp cotton swab.

It stung for a moment, and Marla flinched.

The nurse smiled at her. "You're being very brave. Now I'll cut a bandage for it."

Marla watched Ms. Newman unroll a piece of gauze and snip it with the scissors.

Then she dropped the gauze and gripped Marla's arm. "This won't hurt a bit," Ms. Kramer promised.

"Huh?" Marla said, confused. "What's going on?"

Ms. Kramer raised the scissors high over her head.

Terror froze Marla's muscles. She couldn't move. She stared helplessly at the shining steel scissors and the sharp, glistening points of their blades.

The nurse's eyes glittered like blue ice.

She's changed, Marla thought, swallowing hard. Something else is inside her now.

The Dark Forces.

And she's going to do it. She's going to slit my throat!

Chapter Eighteen

Ms. Kramer pointed the scissors down toward Marla's throat.

"Kill . . . or . . . die!" the nurse roared in an ugly inhuman voice.

The scissors plunged down.

The office door burst open.

"How's the patient, Ms. Kramer?" Mrs. White asked.

The nurse turned to the gym teacher. Her hand opened. She dropped the scissors onto the floor.

Marla watched in amazement as Nurse Kramer smiled at Mrs. White with warm blue eyes.

She's normal again, Marla realized.

"Marla will be fine," Ms. Kramer said. "As soon as I patch up this cut on her neck."

Marla sat up and smiled brightly. "I'm already fine," she said. "Really. I feel great."

Then, without waiting, she jumped off the examining table and raced out of the nurse's office. No way could she stay there. No way she could stay there—and die.

Marla's mind raced as she ran out of the school building.

Kill or die. That's what Ms. Kramer had growled.

But I don't want to die.

I don't want to die!

Marla suddenly felt dizzy. Her stomach churned as she slumped onto the front steps of Shadyside High. She placed her head in her hands as she realized what had to be done.

There was no other way.

Kill . . . or die.

Kenny Klein's house stood at the end of the street, behind a long row of fir trees. Gingerbread trim outlined the porch and shutters. Soft, warm light glowed in the windows.

The streetlights went on as twilight turned to darkness. Marla had been standing on the sidewalk for hours now. Studying the house.

It looked so normal and cheery. The perfect all-American home. A place where people felt safe and happy.

But Marla knew better.

Someone was going to die there tonight.

I have to do it, she realized. I don't have a choice.

They're not giving me a choice.

I'm trapped—and this is my only way out.

Clutching her backpack, she pushed her way past the picket fence and marched to the front porch. She climbed the white wooden steps. Her footsteps thudded heavy and loud.

She raised her hand to ring the doorbell but stopped herself.

Come on, Marla, she thought. You have no choice. No choice . . .

She pressed the doorbell with her finger. A soft chime echoed inside the house.

Marla could feel her heart pounding in her chest. It seemed to grow louder when she heard footsteps inside.

Turn around now, Marla, she told herself. Run away. Don't do this.

The door swung open.

"Marla! What's up?"

Kenny stood in the doorway in cutoff jeans and a T-shirt. His hair was tangled and his eyelids heavy—as if he'd been sleeping.

"Did I—did I wake you up?" Marla asked, her voice catching in her throat. "I'm really sorry. I could come back another time if—"

Kenny yawned. "That's okay. I just dozed off in front of the TV." He rubbed his eyes and stretched. "It's good that you woke me up. I'm supposed to be studying French."

Marla shifted nervously. "That's, uh, that's why I dropped by," she explained. "I thought that maybe you and I could study together. I mean . . ."

Her voice trailed off. Kenny's face lit up.

"Study together? Sure!" he exclaimed. "Come on in!"

He opened the door wider and ushered Marla inside.

"My parents are both working late tonight," he said. "So I've got the house to myself."

Kenny led her into the living room. Marla tried to smile as she lowered herself onto the big, overstuffed sofa. She pulled her notebook out of her bag.

Kenny plopped himself down next to her, kicking his feet up on the large coffee table.

"See?" he said, pointing at the schoolbooks on the table. "I tried to study, but you know how it is. MTV is a little more interesting than French verbs."

Marla laughed—but inside she felt sick.

Kenny flipped open his French book and started reviewing the future tense. Marla stared blankly at his boyish face and sparkling eyes.

He's actually cute, she thought. Really cute. And really nice, too. But I never realized that before. I was too busy competing with him to notice anything.

Marla's head swam with confusion. I can't do this. I can't!

Kill . . . or die, a voice echoed in her brain.

Kenny began talking about the French exam.

But Marla wasn't listening. She felt something inside her go numb. As if some part of her mind had just shut down.

She fixed her gaze on Kenny's throat. She studied his Adam's apple. It bobbed up and down as he spoke.

Then she focused on his windpipe—and concentrated with all her might.

She imagined invisible hands around Kenny's throat, squeezing, squeezing . . .

Squeezing the breath out of him.

Kenny kept talking, reading aloud from a list of practice sentences.

Marla intensified her focus. She no longer felt remorse or sympathy. Or even fear. Something had taken over—the need to end Kenny's life. The need to protect her own life.

A tingling feeling surged through Marla's hands.

The power! she thought. It's working.

She tried to direct the energy to the muscles of Kenny's neck.

She concentrated . . . concentrated . . . using the power to squeeze his throat.

Tighter . . . tighter.

"So how is your neck?" Kenny asked her,

breaking the spell. "I heard about your accident in gym class. Weird. You cut your neck?"

Marla blinked her eyes. The tingling in her hands stopped.

Her hand shot up to her throat. "I—I feel fine," she stammered. "In fact, I'm not sure I need this bandage anymore."

"Let me check it out," Kenny offered, sliding closer on the sofa. He leaned forward and reached for the bandage. Gently he pulled away a corner of the tape.

Marla stared at Kenny's face, only a few inches away from her own. She could feel his warm breath on her throat. And she could see his neck up close.

Marla's hands began to tingle again. But this time they felt hot. Red hot.

The power was strangling him.

And Kenny was starting to choke.

First his face turned red. Then his eyes rolled back in his head. He flopped back onto the sofa, his chest heaving.

He couldn't breathe!

It's working, Marla realized. I'm doing it.

Kenny gasped for air. His arms frantically thrashed. He motioned desperately to Marla to help him.

Marla sat in silence.

She watched. Waited.

Kenny's face turned a darker shade of red. Tears formed in his eyes.

He was choking now. Grasping his throat. Strangling . . . strangling.

Marla knew she should be feeling something. But a strange, heavy numbness had swept over her. The evil . . . the evil . . .

Kenny shook violently.

Marla felt a surge of power rush through her body like a bolt of lightning.

"Kill him!" a voice in her brain ordered.

"Yes," Marla murmured, in a low, dead voice she didn't recognize. "Yes, I will obey."

And then, without realizing it, without even thinking, Marla began to chant: "Blood is the life. Blood is the power. Blood feeds the earth. Blood is the nourishment of the Dark Ones!"

Kill him! the voice instructed. *Kill him now!*

Like a wild animal, she threw herself on top of Kenny. "Blood is the life!"

Kill him! Kill him!

"Blood is the power. . . ." Marla grabbed Kenny by the throat. "Blood feeds the earth. . . ."

KILLLLLLLLLL HIMMMMMMMMM!

"Blood is the nourishment of the Dark Ones!" Marla cried at the top of her lungs.

Chapter Nineteen

Marla's fingers closed tightly around Kenny's neck.

Then something dark and powerful snapped inside her mind.

The numbness lifted.

The screaming voice disappeared.

Marla froze. She felt herself returning.

Felt the power fading.

What am I doing? she thought in a daze.

With a startled cry she pulled her hands from Kenny's throat.

Kenny fell back against the sofa, still gasping for air. The blood had drained from his face. His eyes rolled in his head.

"Kenny!" Marla cried. "Are you all right? Kenny, please! Don't die! Can you breathe?"

Kenny took several deep breaths, then

opened his eyes. He stared at Marla in shock—and in horror.

"Why?" he uttered, panting and trembling. "Why did you do that, Marla? Why did you try to . . . kill me?"

Marla lowered her head in shame. Then she glanced back at Kenny, her eyes filled with tears.

"It was the power," she said, choking on her words. "The power of the Dark Forces."

Kenny stared at her as if she were crazy. "What are you talking about?" A look of confusion and fear flashed across his face.

Marla knew she had to tell Kenny the truth, tell him everything. Every horrible detail.

"I signed a pact in blood—" she began.

"In blood?" Kenny cut in. "What kind of pact?"

"A pact that joined me to the Dark Forces of the earth—and to those two creepy girls, Roxanne and Elena. We were . . . sort of like a witches' coven."

"Witches?" Kenny exclaimed. "Are you out of your mind? Sorry. Stupid question. Of course you're out of your mind! You just tried to strangle me!"

"Look, I know it all sounds crazy, but I can prove it," Marla said, reaching for her bag. "Here."

She pulled out the pact and handed the yellowed parchment to Kenny.

He squinted as he studied the strange, looping letters—and Marla's bloody signature.

"It's written in a lost language," Marla pointed out.

Kenny stared at the parchment, shaking his head. "Weird," he muttered. "I don't even recognize the alphabet!"

"Roxanne and Elena told me I couldn't read the pact," Marla murmured as Kenny stared at it.

"What else did they tell you?" Kenny asked, setting the pact on the coffee table.

"They told me that the pact demanded blood for blood," Marla explained. "They said if I didn't kill someone, the Dark Forces would kill me."

Kenny gasped. His eyes locked on Marla's. "This is for real, isn't it?" he asked her softly.

Marla nodded. "It's real," she whispered. "And it's so evil."

She buried her face in her hands. She wanted to run away and hide forever. But she knew she couldn't.

The evil would find her.

"Why, Marla?" Kenny asked gently. "Why did you do it? Why did you sign the pact in blood?"

Marla couldn't look at him. She felt so ashamed.

But she had to tell him. She owed him that much. She almost killed him.

"I . . . I wanted to be class valedictorian," she said quietly. "I wanted to be successful . . . like my mom. But no matter what I did—no matter how hard I tried—it wasn't good enough. I'm a failure!"

Marla started to cry. Kenny slid a comforting arm around her shoulders.

"Then everyone started teasing me at school," Marla sobbed. "Everything went wrong. Everybody laughed at me. I couldn't take it. I wanted to scream. I wanted revenge. . . ."

Her voice trembled as Kenny stroked her hair.

"But I never wanted it to go this far," Marla finished her thought.

She looked up at Kenny. "I'm so sorry," she broke down. "I'm sorry that I wanted to hurt you. I'm sorry for everything. But how can you ever forgive me?" She turned away from him.

Kenny pulled her closer. He rubbed her shoulders and whispered in her ear. "It's okay, Marla. I understand. You were under a lot of pressure. Everybody was being mean to you. I teased you, too, just like everyone else."

Why was he being so kind to her? Why didn't he hate her for what she'd done?

"You tried to be nice." Marla gulped. "But I wouldn't let you. I made you my enemy. And then I—I . . . tried to kill you! But I had to! It's in the pact!"

Kenny ran a hand through his hair and leaned over the coffee table. "I have some old books on witchcraft. My dad used to study it.

Maybe we can find something useful in them, Marla. Maybe there's a loophole. Or maybe those girls were lying to you."

Marla dried her eyes. She felt the first glimmer of hope. "You think there's a way out of this?"

"I don't know," Kenny told her. "But we have to find out."

They skimmed through the old books for nearly an hour. Finally Kenny turned to her. "I think those girls were lying," he told Marla.

Marla slammed an old book shut. "Why do you say that?"

"None of the old witchcraft pacts required murder. Look through these books. None of them said anything about *having* to kill."

"You're right," Marla agreed. "According to this book, once you sign the pact in blood, you have the power. But you don't owe the Dark Forces anything."

Kenny gazed at her thoughtfully. "You might be safe. You might be okay."

"But why did Roxanne and Elena lie to me?" Marla asked. "Why would they want me to kill someone?"

"So you'd never leave their circle," Kenny suggested. "When you joined them, Roxanne and Elena became much stronger. They need you, Marla, for your power. And I bet they're willing to do anything to keep you in the circle."

Marla's face flushed with anger.

"They told me the Dark Forces would kill me if I left them," she muttered. "The glowing letters in my bedroom, those sharp pains, the accident in gym class, the school nurse trying to kill me—I thought it was the work of the Dark Forces. When it was really Roxanne and Elena."

"Sounds like it," Kenny agreed. "But that means they're pretty powerful. The stuff they've pulled on you isn't exactly from a cheap magic show."

Marla's heart pounded hard against her chest. She clenched her fists.

"Those creeps!" she shouted. "Those evil, conniving, lying . . ." She struggled to find a word. "Witches!"

She jumped up from the sofa and bolted for the door.

"Marla! Wait!" Kenny yelled after her. "We should read more! We haven't finished—"

But it was too late. Marla stomped out the door, down the porch steps, and into the night.

Midnight in the Fear Street woods.

Marla kept to the darkest shadows. She moved silently through the thick trees and bushes. In the distance she heard chanting.

Soft voices, chanting in a language she didn't recognize.

She tiptoed along the moonlit path near the

wide clearing in the middle of the woods. She peered through a leafy tree branch—and saw them.

Marla watched as the two girls raised their hands above a blazing bonfire. The orange light cast a sinister glow across their pale faces and long black robes. They chanted in unison.

I have to take them by surprise, Marla thought.

She closed her eyes and concentrated. Waiting until her hands started tingling. Until she felt the power surging through her.

Then she stepped into the clearing.

A twig snapped under her foot.

Roxanne and Elena stopped chanting.

Their heads spun around, and their fiery eyes fixed upon Marla.

They didn't seem very glad to see her.

Don't let them scare you, Marla told herself.

Gathering her courage, she marched toward the fire.

"What are you doing here?" Roxanne snarled. "What do you want?"

"Guess," Marla snapped back.

Elena giggled nervously. "You probably want revenge. That's perfect. That's what we're doing," she whispered, eyes glowing. "Helping you get revenge against the senior class."

Marla narrowed her eyes at them angrily. "No," she fumed. "I want revenge . . . against you!"

Roxanne and Elena froze in surprise.

"You told me I had to kill Kenny," Marla went on. "You just wanted me to kill someone so that you could keep me for the rest of my life. So that I'd be bound to the circle. To help you with your own sick magic."

"Wait. Listen to us for a minute," Roxanne broke in.

"Why should I?" Marla asked furiously. "You're both liars. You told me I had to kill someone because it was in the pact."

"It *is* in the pact!" Elena protested.

"Then I guess you didn't read it closely," Marla said.

"We can't read it," Roxanne reminded her. "It's written in a lost language!"

"That doesn't matter. There are hundreds of books about the ancient Dark Arts!" Marla told them. "I read through several of them tonight. And now I know the truth. I don't owe you—or the Dark Forces—anything! You don't have any power over me!"

A wicked grin flashed across Roxanne's face. "Maybe not," she said. "Which means we can't afford to keep you around any longer."

"Fine," Marla said. "Believe me, I don't intend to hang out with you either."

"That's not what she meant," Elena said.

"What I meant is that we don't have any choice," Roxanne explained softly, without any emotion at all. "Now we have to kill you."

Chapter Twenty

Roxanne and Elena stared over Marla's shoulder.

Something rustled behind Marla. Fear gripped her throat. She turned—and gasped.

The clearing had grown smaller.

The trees were moving in all around her!

Marla quickly scanned the woods for a way to escape.

But the small circle of trees closed in. Their branches waved in the moonlight like monstrous arms.

"There is no escape," Roxanne told her, as if reading her mind.

"No escape," Elena repeated.

Something cracked and splintered over Marla's head. She raised her eyes to see a fat tree branch soar through the air like an arrow.

Marla ducked. The sharp tips of the branch brushed her face. She stood up—and felt another tree branch lash out at her. Her face stung from the blow.

Use the power, Marla told herself. Fight back.

Her hands tingled with unearthly heat. She imagined herself holding an invisible shield—her only defense against the attacking trees. A branch fell lifeless to the ground in front of her feet.

Yes! It's working! Marla thought triumphantly.

Roxanne and Elena lifted a boulder off the ground—and sent it hurtling at her.

Marla's shield didn't stand a chance.

The big rock sailed through the air.

And struck Marla in the chest.

The force knocked the wind out of her. Falling backward, she landed in the dirt with a heavy thud. The boulder rolled across her invisible shield and slammed to the ground beside her.

Roxanne and Elena cackled with delight.

"Stand up, Marla!" Roxanne commanded. "Stand up and face your fate."

Drained of her power, Marla dragged herself to her feet.

It's useless, she realized. They're so much stronger than I am.

She glared at the two girls. "What are you

going to do to me?" she asked defiantly.

"What has to be done," Elena answered.

Roxanne smiled. "We have no choice."

Marla couldn't speak.

She glanced nervously at the woods around her. The trees looked normal again. And the clearing was wide open.

Run, she told herself. Now's your chance.

But she couldn't move.

Her feet felt planted to the ground. A strange, prickly warmth surged through her body. Beads of sweat trickled down her forehead.

What is happening to me?

She stared at Roxanne and Elena. They had joined hands and were mumbling in unison.

Their eyes were fixed on Marla. She could feel their concentration.

They're using the power on me, Marla realized.

A terrible heat began to consume her body. Hotter and hotter, her skin burned with a scalding fever.

She felt as if her body were melting.

"Stop it!" Marla screamed. "Stop it!" She collapsed into a pile of dried leaves.

Roxanne and Elena smiled—and kept on chanting.

Marla howled in pain.

Sweat streamed down her face, her neck. I—I'm boiling! she thought.

My blood—my whole body—boiling! Boiling!

I'm being cooked alive, Marla realized.

In one agonizing moment the fever completely overwhelmed her. Her brain swelled up inside her head, pushing hard against her skull. Her insides bubbled and burned.

Marla raised her arm and stared in horror as steam rose up from her bright-red flesh.

"Make it stop!" she begged. "I don't want to die like this! I'd rather freeze to death!"

Roxanne and Elena stopped chanting.

They shot a wicked look at each other, then crossed their arms and rejoined hands.

Marla's body temperature dropped almost immediately.

She sighed with relief.

Her blood cooled. The sweat on her skin felt soothing in the night air.

I'm going to live, she thought.

But then she saw that Roxanne and Elena were chanting again. A new spell?

Marla's body temperature dropped swiftly. Lower, lower . . .

Until she started to shiver.

I'm freezing, Marla thought.

A chill swept through Marla's body. Her spine stiffened and froze. Her teeth chattered. The sweat on her skin turned to ice.

Colder.

Marla's lips trembled, then turned blue. She tried to cry out, but she couldn't.

Her mouth and throat were frozen shut.

So cruel, she thought.

How can the two of them be so cruel?

Her mind reeled to a halt. Her thoughts seemed to freeze up along with her body. Even her heart thudded to a grinding, slow beat.

Roxanne and Elena uncrossed their hands. They broke off their chant and turned to Marla. Elena tapped Marla's cheek with her finger.

"Frozen solid," the dark-haired girl gloated. "You don't happen to have an ice pick on you, do you?"

Roxanne laughed.

The two girls leaned forward and studied Marla's eyes.

Marla stared back blankly.

"Don't worry, Marla," Roxanne whispered. "Your nerves are frozen. You won't feel a thing. In fact, your brain must be numb. Can you even hear what I'm saying?"

Marla heard her, all right. But she couldn't answer back.

Her mind was fading. Dying.

"Bye-bye," Roxanne whispered.

Then Marla disappeared as a deep, cold darkness swept over her.

Chapter Twenty-one

"**M**arla . . ." a voice called out to her in
the darkness.
Then a hand touched her. An arm
wrapped around her shoulders.

It's death, Marla thought. The cold hug of
death.

But no.

Its touch was warm. Its voice was human.

"Come on, Marla. The fire will warm you up."

She felt a wave of heat on her face. Soft
hands began to rub her arms and shoulders.
Slowly Marla felt her whole body thawing.

The icy chill began to fade.

"Marla? Talk to me!"

Her eyes fluttered. Her vision cleared. She
found herself staring into the leaping flames of
a bonfire. She turned her head and saw Kenny.

"Marla! You're awake!" he cheered. "How do you feel? Can you talk?"

Marla cleared her throat. She opened her mouth. "Y-Yes," she managed to say. "Kenny, what—"

"I followed you here," Kenny broke in. "When you ran out of my house. I was worried about you."

Marla shook her head. "You shouldn't have come, Kenny," she said softly. "Roxanne and Elena . . . they're too dangerous. They'll kill you."

Kenny pulled her closer, resting her head on his shoulder. "I couldn't stand the thought of something happening to you," he replied.

Marla lifted her head and stared into Kenny's eyes.

His face drew closer to hers, and Marla closed her eyes.

They kissed.

Marla felt the warmth of Kenny's lips. It seemed to spread throughout her entire body.

Their lips parted. Marla opened her eyes and smiled.

"Kenny," she whispered.

"Shhhh." He cradled her gently in his arms. The whole world seemed to fade away.

Nothing existed—except the night, and the woods, and the crackling fire.

And Kenny.

Marla sighed. For the first time in her life,

she felt happy and safe.

An ember popped in the bonfire.

Marla jumped—and the nightmare came rushing back to her.

"What am I going to do about Roxanne and Elena?" she asked, feeling a sudden wave of panic.

"They think you're dead," Kenny pointed out. "We can use it to our advantage."

Marla looked up in surprise. "What are you talking about—*our* advantage? This is *my* problem. I don't want you to get involved."

"I'm already involved, Marla," Kenny told her. "And I have a plan."

Chapter Twenty-two

Marla didn't show her face at school the next day.

But she was there. Watching. Waiting. Hiding in a small, crowded closet that the school used to store textbooks.

I hope Kenny knows what he's doing, she thought. I feel as if I'm trapped inside a coffin.

Marla tried to angle her stiff shoulders in the cramped space. No matter how she positioned herself, she couldn't get comfortable. At least there were little air vents in the door, she thought.

What time is it? she wondered. Homeroom should be over by now.

Marla sighed with relief when the bell rang. She heard the voices of kids laughing and talking in the hallway.

Marla peered through one of the vents and waited.

Finally they appeared in the hallway. Roxanne and Elena.

And Kenny, too.

He stopped the two girls in front of the storage closet. "Wait up, you two," he called to them. "I need to talk to you."

Roxanne and Elena turned and stared at Kenny with hatred in their eyes.

"What do *you* want?" Roxanne snarled.

Kenny lowered his voice. "I know everything," he said bluntly.

Roxanne didn't blink. "What are you talking about? What do you know?"

"About the pact," Kenny explained. "About the pact that Marla signed."

Roxanne and Elena rolled their eyes.

Elena sighed. "Marla is history."

Kenny smiled. "Yes, I know. That's why I want to talk to you. I want to join your circle."

The two girls scoffed. "Get a life," Roxanne jeered. She and Elena started walking away.

"I have the power," Kenny announced.

Roxanne and Elena froze. They spun around and eyed him up and down.

"Prove it," Roxanne challenged.

That's my cue, Marla thought from her hiding place.

She stared through the vent and concentrated on Roxanne's shoulder bag. Her hands tingled with the power.

This had better work, she thought, staring at the bag, calling on the power.

Roxanne's shoulder bag flew into the air. It slammed against a locker and fell to the floor. Makeup and other items spilled across the tiles.

Roxanne and Elena stared at Kenny in amazement.

"He did it!" Elena gasped. "He's got the power!"

Roxanne studied Kenny. "I'm impressed," she said.

"Impressed? I'm totally shocked!" Elena exclaimed. "Wow. You're a real find."

Roxanne moved close to Kenny and whispered in his ear. "Join us tonight. At midnight. Go to the clearing in the middle of the Fear Street woods."

Roxanne scooped her things back into her bag. Then she stood up and walked away, chatting excitedly with Elena.

Kenny casually leaned against the closet door.

"Tonight," he whispered in to Marla. "Tonight they're dead."

The moon rose, full and round, above the jagged treetops of the Fear Street woods. A soft orange light glowed in the heart of the forest—an arc of candles, a bubbling bowl on an altar covered with a red velvet cloth.

Two hooded figures stood near the fire. They chanted as they added more ingredients to the mixture.

Marla and Kenny crouched down in the bushes by the edge of the clearing. Silently they watched Roxanne and Elena chant as they placed ingredients into the silver bowl.

"They're preparing the summoning elixir." Marla grabbed Kenny's hand. "They're going to do it," Marla whispered. "They're going to open up a crack in the earth."

"That will be our signal," Kenny said, nodding. "You push Elena into the pit. I'll take care of Roxanne."

Marla bit her lip.

Kenny glanced at his watch. "It's midnight," he announced. "Time to party."

He stood up. Marla held on to his hand. "Be careful," she whispered.

"You, too," Kenny whispered back. He startled her by lifting her hand and kissing it. Then he took a deep breath—and marched off into the clearing.

Roxanne and Elena glanced up. Their faces gleamed in the firelight.

Please, be careful, Kenny, she prayed silently.

Kenny approached the two hooded figures. "Hey, what's cooking?" he joked.

The girls didn't laugh.

Marla's heart started racing.

Something's wrong, she thought. They should be welcoming him.

She held her breath and listened.

"Well, look who's here," Roxanne crooned. "And I thought he was supposed to be the senior brain."

"For someone who gets straight A's, he's kind of stupid," Elena added.

The two girls burst into scornful laughter.

Kenny appeared stunned. "Whoa. What do you mean?"

"You thought we'd fall right into your trap!" Roxanne sneered. "That was so lame, Kenny. We knew Marla was hiding in the storage closet this morning. Did you think we couldn't feel her power?"

Kenny's mouth dropped open, but no sound came out.

"You actually thought we'd let you join our circle?" Elena teased. "Sorry, Kenny, but we have other plans for you."

"What . . . what are talking about?" Kenny stammered.

"Blood sacrifice," Roxanne answered. "It increases our power like you wouldn't believe."

"Marla was supposed to kill you," Elena explained. "We thought she was ambitious enough to be part of our circle. We thought she'd have a real talent for this."

Roxanne rolled her eyes. "I knew that stuck-up wimp wouldn't go through with it. She's probably hiding out in the bushes right now, shaking like a leaf!"

Marla gasped and ducked down. Roxanne was pointing straight at her!

Do something, Marla, she ordered herself. *Now.*

But her mind went blank with panic.

"I'm glad Marla didn't kill you, Kenny," Roxanne said, moving closer to him. "Because now I'll have the pleasure of killing you myself!"

Marla froze. She stared in helpless horror as Elena grabbed Kenny by the arm. Kenny staggered forward.

Then Roxanne pulled the ceremonial knife from her robes.

And pointed the tip at Kenny's chest.

arla screamed as the knife lowered toward Kenny's chest.

Roxanne smiled with evil glee.

Marla concentrated on the knife. Burn, she thought with all her might. *Burn!*

Her hands tingled with energy.

Roxanne howled in pain and dropped the knife. She clutched her hand, shaking it. "Owww. It burns!"

Marla cheered silently.

Kenny shoved Elena to the ground and charged toward the woods.

Roxanne raised her hand and chanted.

A tree root burst up from the ground. Grabbed Kenny by the ankle—and dragged him down.

"Marla!" he shouted. "Run!"

But Marla wouldn't run.

I got you into this, Kenny, she thought. And I'm going to get you out. Alive.

She stared hard at Elena. The short, frizzy-haired girl was climbing to her feet over a large crack in the ground.

The spot where the earth had opened up during my initiation, Marla remembered.

That's it! I have to open up the pit! she thought.

But what are the words that do it? Marla couldn't remember.

Think, Marla, think!

She didn't have much time. Roxanne was running through the trees toward her.

"Peekaboo," Roxanne taunted her. She pointed a finger. "I see you, Marla. And in a few seconds I'm going to see you die!"

A tree branch shot out at Marla. It lashed across her right arm and coiled around her wrist.

Marla screamed.

Another branch grabbed her left arm, pulling her in the opposite direction.

Then two fingerlike roots reached up from the earth. They wrapped around her ankles.

The branches tightened their grasp on her legs—and yanked hard. Cut through her skin.

Marla shrieked in agony.

Roxanne laughed. She moved to a willow tree and broke off a long, slender branch. She cracked it in the air like a whip.

Marla searched for Kenny.

A dozen tree roots pinned him on his back to the ground. He cried out as he struggled desperately to free himself.

In the middle of the clearing Elena crawled to her feet. "Kill them, Roxanne!" she shouted. "Kill them both!"

Roxanne raised the tree branch and swung it at Marla's face. The sharp tip grazed her cheek.

Marla turned her head away.

"You should have played by our rules, Marla," Roxanne said through gritted teeth. "We wanted to help you. We wanted to be your friends."

"I'd rather be dead," Marla shot back.

Roxanne smiled grimly, raising her right hand.

A bright shiny object flew through the air and landed in Roxanne's palm.

The ceremonial knife.

Marla shuddered, watching the silver blade gleam in the moonlight.

Roxanne stepped forward, brandishing the knife. "I'm going to take your power, Marla," she said. "You don't know how to use it. You don't *deserve* it. I'm going to take your power from you."

Marla refused to show how frightened she was. "How are you going to do that?" she demanded.

Roxanne's eyes flashed in the moonlight. "I'm going to cut out your heart," she answered, "and eat it."

She took a step closer to Marla. She raised the knife and pressed the tip against Marla's chest.

"No!" Marla gasped, struggling. She felt the pressure of the blade against her pounding chest.

Think fast! she told herself. Try to remember those words! Open the pit!

She closed her eyes. "Spirits of Earth, Spirits of Darkness, answer my call—" she began.

The earth trembled and heaved.

Surprised, Roxanne stumbled back. She tripped over a rock. Fell to the ground.

Marla saw the rocks and trees begin to shake violently.

Her body swayed as the whole world rocked back and forth. "Open the darkness! Open the darkness! Open the darkness!" she yelled into the night.

The trees pitched wildly back and forth. Marla felt the branches loosen around her ankles and wrists. She slipped away and scrambled toward Kenny.

"Kenny—I'm coming!" she cried out.

Across the clearing Kenny struggled under the tree roots. Finally he pulled himself free and staggered toward Marla.

The forest rumbled.

Then Marla heard a scream from the middle of the clearing.

Elena! Her body rocked from side to side. The earth swelled up beneath her.

A wide crack split the ground open. Elena's feet disappeared into the earth. She clawed at the dirt with both hands. Tongues of flame shot up around her.

The crevice widened—and swallowed her up.

"Noooooo!" Elena's shrieks echoed in the fiery chasm like a distant siren.

Then—silence.

Kenny rushed to Marla's side. "Marla! You did it!"

He hugged her tight.

Marla glanced nervously across the clearing. The pit yawned like a giant mouth. A flame shot up from its depths.

Then the woods were quiet.

Too quiet.

Marla scanned the area.

"Where's Roxanne?" she whispered in Kenny's ear.

Kenny narrowed his eyes, searching the trees. "She must have run away," he said softly. "You scared her off, Marla! You opened up the pit! You destroyed Elena! You did it!"

"Yes, you did!" a harsh voice rang out from above.

Marla froze in Kenny's arms.

They both peered up at the sky.

Roxanne hovered in the air over their heads.

She stared down at them. An evil green flame flickered in her eyes.

"You killed my best friend," she said. "Now, Marla, it's *my* turn for revenge!"

Chapter Twenty-four

Floating above them, Roxanne gripped the ceremonial knife with both hands.

She let out a piercing scream, a scream of fury—and swooped down.

"Go!" Kenny shouted. He pushed Marla toward the woods. Turned and darted in the other direction, heading for the center of the clearing.

Marla saw Roxanne hesitate for a moment, trying to decide which victim to follow.

She chose Kenny.

"Kenny! Look out!" Marla shrieked.

Roxanne soared after him. She glided over the ground, her robes flapping in the wind.

Kenny scrambled toward a pile of dead wood near the open pit.

He grabbed a thick branch—and dipped it

into the dancing flames from the pit.

Roxanne dived.

Kenny swung around. Raised the burning tree branch like a torch.

Roxanne tried to stop.

Too late.

Kenny thrust the flaming branch in her face.

In the light of the yellow flame Marla saw Roxanne's eyes grow wide with horror. And then, as she caught fire, Roxanne opened her mouth in a furious roar that shook the trees.

Marla watched the hood of Roxanne's robe burst into flames. And then her long blond hair ignited into a sizzling ball of fire and sparks.

Thick, black smoke choked the air.

Roxanne collapsed to the ground, shrieking, flames dancing all around her.

Marla gasped in horror. She ran to join Kenny. "You—you did it," she whispered. "She would have killed us both."

Kenny opened his mouth to answer—but stopped.

They both gaped as Roxanne's shrieks of pain turned into howls of laughter.

With one hand Roxanne tore the charred hood and burnt hair from her head. Her exposed scalp smoked and bubbled.

Her face glowed with an angry red intensity.

Roxanne turned her bubbling, bald head—and glared at Marla with ice-blue eyes.

Marla uttered a horrified moan. Her knees

started to collapse. She couldn't move.

Roxanne's stare—it's paralyzing me! Marla realized.

Do something, Marla told herself. Use the power.

She tried to concentrate. But her powers seemed exhausted. No energy surged through her body. Her hands didn't tingle at all.

Roxanne stepped calmly away from the flaming cloak. Her bald head bubbled and steamed. She bent down to retrieve the ceremonial knife.

Slowly she stood. The moonlight gleamed on her burned scalp.

"Enough, Marla," she said, waving the knife in the air. "Fun time is over. Let's get serious."

Marla tried to run. Her feet were stuck to the ground. She lowered her gaze—and gasped. Two tree roots pinned her to the ground.

Marla watched in horror as Roxanne strode calmly toward her. Roxanne raised the blade. Pointed it at Marla's heart.

And began another strange chant.

Marla heard Kenny groan beside her. With a burst of strength he lurched forward—and tackled Roxanne.

Roxanne collapsed beneath him. The knife flew from her hand—and landed at Marla's feet.

Grabbing the knife, Marla slashed at the tree roots that pinned her feet.

Hacking . . . hacking . . . slashing frantically at the thick roots. Finally she freed herself. Panting like a wild animal, she jumped away.

And dived toward Kenny and Roxanne, who were in a furious wrestling match, rolling over the grass, punching and gouging at each other.

Roxanne heaved Kenny away. Kenny rolled to the edge of the fiery pit.

"Noooo!" Marla wailed.

The power tingled in her hands. A burst of unearthly energy surged through her body.

Roxanne rose to her feet. "You're dead, Marla!" she roared. "First I'll kill you. Then I'll torture him. You'll both pay for killing Elena!"

Roxanne raised her hands and chanted.

Marla concentrated. She braced herself for the attack.

Then an eerie wail rose from the pit. "*Roxxxxaaannnnne!*"

Roxanne stopped chanting. "It's Elena!" she cried.

"*Roxanne, help me!*" Elena's plea rose up from somewhere deep in the earth. "*Please— don't leave me in here!*"

Marla watched Roxanne race to the edge of the chasm. "Elena, hold on!" she cried. "I'm going to get you out."

It worked! Marla thought.

I used my powers to make Elena's voice come from the pit. I tricked Roxanne. She believes it is her friend calling to her.

Now Marla had to act fast.

She took a deep breath. Then rushed up behind Roxanne—and shoved her deep into the bottomless pit.

Chapter Twenty-five

Her chest heaving, her entire body trembling violently, Marla perched at the edge of the pit, gazing into its fiery depths.

Roxanne screamed all the way down. A scream of agony that echoed off the chasm walls until it became a thousand screams.

"Marla?" She heard Kenny behind her. "Marla . . . you saved us." His arms slid around her.

Marla sighed. "How come I don't feel thrilled?" she said wearily. Then answered her own question. "Because I killed two people."

"They were evil," Kenny replied. "They were murderers. Someone had to stop them."

"Murderers," Marla whispered. She shuddered. "They would have killed us both."

Kenny tugged her gently. "Come on," he said. "We should go."

Marla let herself lean against him.

Her mother always told her she had to be totally self-sufficient. That a successful woman could depend only on herself. That only weak people leaned on others.

So why, Marla wondered, did this feel so right?

They started from the clearing together.

But a thundering sound made Marla turn back. A huge tongue of flame burst out of the pit with a deafening roar.

Marla staggered back, shielding her eyes.

An explosion of fire lit up the night sky. The flames touched the treetops, then slipped back into the darkness of the pit.

Marla grabbed Kenny's hand. "It's going to be okay," she whispered.

The ground trembled. The crevice shrank.

And the pit closed.

Chapter Twenty-six

Marla squinted against the bright sunlight as she approached Shadyside High. The sight of the school filled her with joy—even though today was the day of the French final exam.

After fighting the Forces of Darkness, taking a French test seemed like a piece of cake!

Smiling to herself, Marla stepped up to the new front door of the school. She felt a sudden pang of guilt, remembering what happened to Josie.

Opening the door, Marla hurried into the front hall. As she headed for her locker, she was so glad to be back, she felt like dancing!

"Hey, Matty! Mickey! What's up with you guys?" she called out cheerfully.

She grinned at their expressions of surprise.

"What's up with you?" Mickey replied.

Marla stopped. "Hey—how about a truce? Getting in each other's faces is getting kind of old, right?"

Matty looked confused. But he shrugged and said, "Okay. Whatever."

And Mickey told her, "You know, you're not half bad for someone who's perfect."

"You're so kind," Marla replied, and crossed the hall to her locker.

"Marla, wait up!"

Marla turned in surprise to see Clarissa Turner running toward her.

"Hey!" Clarissa called.

"Hey," Marla echoed.

Clarissa seemed nervous. "Look," she began. "I just wanted to tell you maybe I had you wrong. I mean, I told Josie you asked about her, that you were worried about her. I told her how nice you were, even though you and she don't get along. I don't know if Josie believed me. . . ."

Marla shrugged. "It could take a while to convince her."

"Like a lifetime." Clarissa sighed.

"But you and I are okay?" Marla asked. "I'm really sorry for all the obnoxious things I said."

Clarissa smiled. "Me, too. I think it's pretty equal between us."

"Clarissa, where've you been?" Trisha called out. She and Jennifer came walking up the hall.

Jennifer shot Marla a suspicious look. "Everything okay?" she asked Clarissa.

"Everything's fine," Clarissa answered. "I was just going to ask Marla if she wanted to get some pizza with us after school. If she's not busy studying, that is."

Marla grinned. "Don't tell my mother, but even I get the occasional afternoon off."

"Great," Clarissa said. "Catch you later."

Marla waved good-bye. She turned to her locker and spun open the combination lock. She grabbed some books. Then she slammed the door shut.

Hearing someone call her name, she spun around.

"Josie!" she cried. "You're back from the hospital! How do you feel?"

Josie shrugged. "Not bad. Not great. But not bad. I'm all patched up—look!"

She pulled her dark bangs away from her face.

"See?" she asked. "Check it out. It's all pretty much healed up."

Marla examined Josie's forehead. Her skin looked pink and smooth—except for a few tiny scratches.

"That looks like it's going to be as good as new," Marla said thankfully.

Josie dropped her hair back into place. "Hey, Marla—thanks for sending those flowers while I was in the hospital. It was really sweet of you—especially after I pulled that joke on you."

Marla shrugged. "Don't worry about it," she said. "I'm just glad you're okay."

The first bell rang, and she hurried toward her homeroom. Everything is back to normal, she thought. Actually, it's even better than it was. Except for having a French final.

After history class Marla waited for Kenny on the front steps of the school. She hadn't seen him all day.

Where is he? Marla wondered. He wasn't in history, and last night he told me to meet him here. She glanced at her watch. We have to take the French final in a few minutes.

Marla fingered the chain around her neck— and Kenny's class ring. He had given it to her the night before.

Marla still couldn't believe that the worst disaster of her life had turned into a romance.

She checked her watch again. I should go inside. Kenny isn't showing. I can't be late for the final.

"Marla!"

She turned.

Waving his arms, Kenny came jogging up the steps toward her.

"Kenny! Where've you been?" Marla called out. "We're going to be late."

Kenny caught up with her. His face was

flushed with excitement—and something else that Marla recognized.

Fear.

"Kenny?" she said softly. "What's wrong?"

Kenny leaned down with his hands on his knees and caught his breath. When he straightened up, all the color had drained from his face.

"The pact!" he said breathlessly. "I read more about it last night after I got home."

"Huh? More?" Marla's voice caught in her throat. "But, Kenny—those girls are gone. We're through with all of that. Why—?"

"I—I'm not sure," he stammered.

A chill swept down Marla's back. "What do you mean?" she gasped, grabbing his arm. "What did you read? Tell me the truth, Kenny."

Kenny sighed. "The book says . . . if you ever use your powers to kill another of your kind— if you kill someone else who practices the Dark Arts—then . . ."

His voice trailed off.

"Then *what*, Kenny? Tell me!" Marla pleaded.

Kenny stared down at the steps. "Then you die—exactly twelve hours later."

Marla's mouth dropped open. A tiny cry escaped her throat.

Then a cold silence seemed to fall over the world.

Kenny was saying something to her. But Marla couldn't hear him.

She could hear only the pounding of her heart.

And then the rumbling of the ground.

"No! No—please—!" She gasped, staggering back.

The steps of the school trembled.

"No! Please!"

With a deafening grinding sound, the concrete steps split open.

"Please, no—!"

The ground split open.

"Noooo!"

Marla reached for Kenny.

Too late.

A swarm of thick, black roots reached up from the pit, snapping like claws.

They grabbed Marla around the waist.

And dragged her down.

R.L. Stine
Seniors
a FEAR STREET series

available from Gold Key® Paperbacks

FEAR STREET® Sagas

available from Gold Key® Paperbacks:

FEAR STREET® titles
available from Gold Key® Paperbacks:

About R.L. Stine

R.L. Stine is the best-selling author in America. He has written more than one hundred scary books for young people, all of them bestsellers.

His series include *Fear Street, Fear Street Seniors,* and the *Fear Street Sagas*.

Bob grew up in Columbus, Ohio. Today he lives in New York City with his wife, Jane, his son, Matt, and his dog, Nadine.

Do you know the address for Fear?

www.fearstreet.com

Connect to the curse of **The Fear Family** with the brand new **Fear Street Website!** This scary site brings you up close and personal with the legend of the Fears and their legacy of blood. With sneak peeks of upcoming stories, top secret information, games, gossip, and the latest buzz from R.L. Stine on who will survive, this is your chance to know the deadly truth.

Get caught in the web of fear!

Don't Miss FEAR STREET® Seniors
Episode Eleven!

PROM DATE

Jennifer Fear has just one wish.

To get a date for the prom. Then she meets Duke.
He's smart, cool, and really hot. Totally perfect!

But Duke isn't as perfect as Jennifer thinks. And now
her dream date is turning into a nightmare.